ANTOINE BANDELE

ORISHAS AMONG MORTALS

COLLECTION 1

This book is a work of fiction with no intent to disrespect or offend the faith systems, religion, and mythology it draws from.

Publisher: Bandele Books
Interior Design: Vellum
Editors: Fiona McLaren, Callan Brown
Illustrator: Arthur Bowling
Cover Design: Mibl Art

ISBN: 978-1-951905-36-1 (eBook)

ISBN: 978-1-951905-38-5 (Hardback)

First Edition | December 8, 2023

WHAT IS TJ YOUNG & THE ORISHAS

The story you're about to read, *Orishas Among Mortals, Collection 1,* is a parallel compilation of tales for the first three books in the *TJ Young & The Orishas* mainline series. *TJ Young & The Orishas* is inspired by the West African mythology of the Orishas.

For suggested and chronological reading order visit: antoinebandele.com/tj-young-timeline

If you enjoy this story and are interested in the rest of its world, you can join Antoine Bandele's e-mail alerts list. He'll send you exclusive behind-the-page content, including art, deleted scenes, and more.

Visit this link:
antoinebandele.com/stay-in-touch

PRONUNCIATION GUIDE

Characters

A·nan·si - ah'nan'see
A·yo·de·ji - eye'o'day'gee
E·shu - eh'shoe
I·be·ji - e'bae'jee
I·fe·da·yo - ee'fey'die'yo
Ma·at - mah'at
Mjol·nir - me'yul'nir
O·ba·ta·la - o'ba'ta'la
O·du·du·wa - oh'doo'doo'wah
O·lo·du·ma·re - o'low'do'ma'ray
O·lo·kun - o'low'koon
O·lo·sa - o'low'sah
O·lo·shi - o'lo'she
O·run·mi·la - o'rune'mee'lah
O·sho·si - oh'show'she
O·shun - o'shoon
O·ya - oi'ya
Shan·go - shawn'go
To·mo·ri Jo·mi·lo·ju - toe'moe'ree joe'mee'low'jew
Ya·ma·ra·ja - yah'mah'rah'jah
Ye·mo·ja - ye'mo'jah
Ye·wa - ye'wah

Terms

A·she - ah'shay
Jo·tunn - yow'tn
Im·pun·du·lu - eem'poon'doo'loo

Locations

La·gos - la'gos
I·jo·ba I·pa·ri - ee'joe'bah ee'pah'ree
U·ten·heim - oo'tin'hi'm

CONTENTS

This story is
a work of fantasy fiction
and not an accurate depiction of
the living practice of Ifa
and its many branches and followers
in the Motherland
and the diaspora.

ANTOINE BANDELE

WILL OF THE MISCHIEF MAKER

WILL OF THE MISCHIEF MAKER

Eshu didn't care what the other Orishas said; the mortals had it right. They had bicycles, trains, cars, and most importantly, planes. Heck, even a sluggish air-balloon would've done the trick, no matter how slow it was. That would've been much better than climbing an endless golden chain to the heavens.

Sprinkles of water dewed Eshu's face and saturated his long, drooping hat. He thought it was the condensation of the clouds that wet him, but as he scaled farther and farther upward, the rushing of waterfalls filled his ears.

It might've been ages since he'd been up there, yet he knew he was close. He knew this not only because his loincloth and hat were getting soaked through, but because the strain in his arms was giving way to fatigue.

A few more grabs, pulls, and lifts later, and Eshu finally broke the plane of the tallest and thickest clouds. And it was about time —the strength in his hold was threatening to leave him, forcing him to tumble back to the Mortal Realm.

Before I get done here, Eshu thought, *I'm going to make some changes to this damn sky chain.*

A collection of floating mountains spread out ahead of him, dotting the deep-blue canvas between the sky and heavens. The water that had ruined Eshu's clothes came flowing from the waterfalls that fell into the clouds to cast rain on the mortals below.

The Orisha grunted and wiped his face clean for the dozenth time. Then, with a long, resounding breath, he lifted himself over the small plot of earth, which served as an anchor for the sky chain.

Eshu took measure of his surroundings. It had been a while since he'd visited the Sky Realm. He remembered then why it had been so long. Everything up here was so ethereal, so peaceful, so perfect.

And absolutely a bore.

That's another thing the mortals got right. They knew how to spice up a place, make it their own. His fellow Orishas, however, especially the ones who lived way up in the clouds, had as much flavor as the human's oatmeal.

Squinting, Eshu surveyed each mountain atop their floating islands. He scanned for a specific peak... a snow-capped range that housed a certain Orisha of interest. And just there, between the sun's ray and the moon's glow, a perfectly angled cap of snow glimmered like a shining pyramid of silver-white.

"*Wà si mi,*" Eshu said, and a staff snapped into his hand from nothingness. He twisted the wooden shaft around his body, and his clothes dried in an instant.

"All right, old friend," he murmured. "Let's see if you're still up there."

With another flourish of his staff, a cluster of clouds gathered around his floating plot of earth. He smiled. Now that he had made the climb, he was free to travel as he pleased, free of the chain that suppressed the full use of his *Ashe*—his magical energy.

He tipped his toe on the first patch of cloud to test his

purchase. When his weight found proper balance, he skipped along the clouds he manifested before him, one by one.

Eshu chuckled the entire way to Obatala's domain.

KNOCK, KNOCK, KNOCK.

Eshu slammed the bulky door knocker against the giant snow-swept doors for the dozenth time.

"Obatala!" he called out through cupped hands. "It's me, Eshu! Your old friend!"

There was no answer.

Eshu pouted in exaggerated annoyance. He didn't come all this way just to be ignored. And had he been any other Orisha, Obatala's cold-shoulder would've stuck, forcing him to return from where he came.

But Eshu wasn't like the others; he was the Gatekeeper, the Master of Thresholds. No path was ever obstructed to him.

It also helped that he was the one who installed the lock on Obatala's door to begin with.

Drawing out his staff once more, Eshu gave the grand doors a light tap. The enormous slabs of birch gave way to Eshu's magic without protest, lumbering inward. Snow dust shook off the opulent doors like a new day of winter, and light spilled into the empty foyer.

Eshu had a hard time keeping his eyes from squinting. Every surface in the tall room blinded him with its grand white staircase, white rugs, white banners, white vases, and white doves—the latter of which glided between the large windows and their wide sills.

"Hello!" Eshu called out once more.

His only response was his own echo.

So then... time to search.

In the Mortal Realm, the palace would've measured the size of a small city. But the daunting task of exploring its many halls, libraries, and chambers was nothing for the Master of Mischief. Every door opened to greet him like an old friend—though none of them offered up who he was looking for. He wasn't rude about it, of course, knocking before entering each room, sometimes with an "Eshu here," or a "the Gatekeeper seeks your audience," or his personal favorite, "is this where they keep the wine?"

Though none of the rooms housed Obatala, Eshu did find several curious items. In one chamber, he discovered a zoo of pale snails sloughing down marble walls; in one of the larger courtyards, he spotted a trio of albino elephants snacking on grass. But most interesting of all was a workshop filled wall-to-wall with ceramics.

The room had all the markings of an inventor's busy hands: loose boards, clay pots completed and in progression, and, of most value to Eshu, the figures of human bodies.

The sight brought a smirk across Eshu's lips. *Good, this should go perfectly.*

He continued onward.

Of course, as such things go, it was the last room Eshu searched that turned out to be the right one. It was at the highest tower in the highest study: Obatala's dream room.

In hindsight, he probably should have checked that one first.

Eshu couldn't tell where the room ended. When he stepped through the doorway, he had to float instead of walk, as there was technically no floor—or at least no floor he could discern far, far below.

Jutting prisms the size of a human movie theater screen studded each wall. And, like a movie screen, they depicted different images, first-person point-of-views of what Eshu assumed were human perspectives. Some of the windows showed a person flying through the sky, others: someone being chased, or people whose teeth were falling out.

"Is that the Gatekeeper I see?" a gentle, yet baritone voice said from above.

Eshu raised his eyes to the endless ceiling to find the giant of a towering Orisha descending upon him. With each passing moment, Obatala reduced in size until he was only slightly taller than Eshu himself.

He doesn't have to do that, Eshu thought.

He didn't mind being small, preferred it even, despite his fellows favoring more colossal builds. Then he remembered how considerate Obatala was. Even if Eshu voiced a complaint, Obatala wouldn't hear it. The ancient Orisha always wanted to put others at ease.

Obatala looked different from what Eshu remembered. How long had it been? A few centuries? A millennium? Whereas before Obatala looked no different from Eshu—save for his typically larger size—now he was devoid of all pigmentation.

Eshu had seen this blight on mortals before. They called it vitiligo, or was it albinism? Wasn't that Obatala's new role now? "*The Shepherd of the Imperfect*," the other Orishas called him.

"I almost didn't recognize you, old friend," Eshu said as Obatala continued to waft in the middle of the grand crystalline room. "Did you do something to your hair?" Eshu had only meant to quip at first, but one of the prisms shined off the distinctly bald head of Obatala's pale skin, a head that was once curtained by long, flowing hair. Now his scalp looked like a pearly bowling ball. "Oh, apparently you did..."

Obatala gave him a kind smirk and an airy chuckle. "It's good to see you too, Gatekeeper. A moment, please?"

He slothed a hand toward Eshu; Eshu glided out of his way.

Behind him, a section of the prism-wall reformed to show a new image: the point-of-view of someone at their desk toiling over complex mathematical equations.

"Whose head are we in right now?" Eshu asked.

Obatala pressed his hands along the fractured image. "This is Doctor Oladipo. He's been trying to work out a cure for glioblastoma."

"A glio—what?"

"A form of cancer."

"Right." Eshu nodded idly. "I always get my cancers mixed up."

Obatala inhaled deeply, then spoke a chant into the wall. With each of his words, the man's pen picked up speed along his notebook.

"He has the information in him," Obatala muttered between chants. "He just needs to manifest it. It's been so hard communing with the mortals. I usually don't work with them when they age past adolescence—they tend to trust in their dreams less and less as they grow. I've not had a breakthrough with one so old since Charles R. Drew decades ago."

"So, why not try communicating with them when they're younger?"

"Oh, I do, as you saw when you entered my domain. But so often the mortal adults ignore those early dreams. And sometimes I'm forced to resort to these... less than perfect circumstances." The scene within the prism changed. The doctor's hands pounded on his desk, and he bunched up his latest piece of paper to discard it.

"Doctor Oladipo always forgets the dreams I send as assistance." Obatala dropped his pale head. "But I can't give up. It's the least I can do for all my wrongs."

"You're not still hung up on *that*, are you?"

Years ago, Obatala had gotten himself drunk when he was charged with the construction of human bodies. He had never forgiven himself for the birth defects and disabilities he caused by his cavalier wine-downs.

"Always." Obatala brushed by Eshu and floated to another portion of the chamber. "You know, Olodumare wouldn't want you traveling between here and the Mortal Realm. I don't even know how you manage it."

"What kind of trickster would I be if I played by the rules? Besides, the Big Guy's been gone for a hot minute now."

"If a 'hot minute' is a few centuries, then yes."

"If you'd visit the mortals from time to time, you'd know the lingo, old friend."

"What are you up to, Gatekeeper?" Obatala cut to the chase with a gentle, curious tone.

"I'll admit it. I'm bored and I'm looking for some company."

"Hah!" Obatala's laugh shook the entire room. "I've never known you to be so easily bored. Have you exhausted all forms of mischief in such brief a time in the Mortal Realm?"

He spun to another prism display. This one showed a cafeteria with the viewer surrounded by a group of children who jeered about the way the child tapped their foot on the corners of the linoleum tiles as they spoke.

"I am trying to help this one gain some social confidence. But more and more, her dreams are tarnished by these other children. Just a few months ago, before starting school, you should have seen the things she was dreaming about. Oh, look! She is transitioning." Obatala's wide and brilliant irises lit up all the brighter. Even in his exclamation his voice was soft and muted. "She is going over Einstein's equations. Not just reciting, but actually forming her own thoughts around it."

"See, friend," Eshu patted Obatala on the shoulder, "where you see faults, I see talent that could never be achieved if this child were born like all the others. How many mortal children do you know who can reform facts as their own thoughts as fast as this one?"

Obatala hummed under his lips. Eshu couldn't tell if the sound was meant to communicate agreement or irritation.

"Tell me," Eshu pried as innocently as possible, "when was the last time you fashioned a human body?"

Obatala shook his head, and a shadow passed over his eyes. "Never again."

"You fear what your hands might make? Well, old friend, I could help you there..." Eshu waved his staff at the nearest prism and reformed an image of Obatala with long hair crafting human bodies. "When's the last time you've tried making a vessel for a non-mortal? One of the Orishas, for example."

Obatala sucked at his teeth and moved around Eshu to another prism. "I knew you came here for a reason. No, Gatekeeper. I will not mold a body for you."

"Come now," Eshu groaned, following along like a pestering child, "it's the only way I can interact with the mortals properly. You, of all of us, should know of the desire to assist them."

"I can't. I refuse."

Okay, so direct questioning wasn't going to do it. Eshu let a silence fall between them as he shifted to a different tack.

"I know what plagues you each day, each season, each era," Eshu began solemnly. "You never got to properly finish your work all that time ago. Not before Oduduwa took over—"

Obatala spun rapidly on Eshu, and the entire chamber darkened like a stormy night. "Never speak that name in my domain."

Eshu threw up his hands. "Of course, of course, excuse me. But think of what you could do! You should have a direct hand in the creation of new human bodies. They could be in the image you truly wanted, what you intended."

Obatala's gaze shifted between another prism and Eshu, seemingly conflicted.

"Listen." Eshu floated in close to Obatala, then murmured, "I'm not asking you to go back to an assembly line. Just one. And for me, not for a human soul."

"Well..." he started to relent, but his pursed lips told of a brewing stubbornness.

Eshu drew in even closer, merely an inch from Obatala's face. "If anything goes wrong, nothing bad will happen. I'll hop out of the body, and you can always try again another time."

"I have wanted to try it out once more..." Obatala said almost to himself. "That much I'll admit."

Eshu careened around Obatala, just at the edge of the Orisha's ear. "Come now. I know what the other Orishas say. I know why you seclude yourself at the highest peaks within the highest clouds. If you made another human body, one of note, none of them could speak against you."

"The Great Monarch hasn't been with us for many ages. I would need his approval to begin with."

Perfect. He was no longer denying his want, no longer denying his capacity to do the task. Now, he was just looking for permission.

And Eshu could give it to him.

"Well, old friend, you are speaking to the Gatekeeper. I'm the next best thing. I saw your workshop coming in—your ceramic work. You've been trying again, haven't you?"

Eshu snapped his fingers, and the room's prisms transformed into the image of Obatala's workshop. "What's that just there?" He nodded to a clay piece in the shape of a bird. "Were you trying with animals first?"

Obatala nodded. "That is the dodo. The humans did away with them decades ago, and I was trying to—No. No, I cannot. I just don't have it in me anymore." He gave Eshu a condoling touch on the shoulder. "Thank you. I appreciate your kind words. But you'll have to go now, old friend."

"You know something, maybe you're right. After all, your best works always came off the back of... liquid inspiration."

"Do not goad me, Gatekeeper. I have been sober for more ages than I can count." Obatala narrowed his bright, pulsating eyes. "If I were to slip back now... who knows what I would do, what I might manifest."

Eshu turned with a shrug. "Ah, I didn't realize you had sworn off the drink like *that.* I might as well do away with this gift I got for you."

Obatala's eyes glinted. "Gift?"

Eshu continued bouncing away from the chamber in a floating skip. "I don't see how my gift could interest someone who claims to be free from liquor."

Obatala sniffed the air. "Is... is that palm wine I smell?"

Eshu beamed as he said, "*Wà si mi,*" and a bottle of milk-white palm wine popped into his hand from thin air. "It even comes in your favorite color. Straight from Osun State."

Obatala stretched out his hand, then drew it back in. Stretched it out once more, then drew it in again. "That's where the Oyo Empire used to be, yes?"

"One and the same. And I'll tell you what, the mortals have gotten even better at fermenting it."

"Oh, I've not had some of that in many, many, ages... not since the Great Monarch's Decree of Separation." He drifted toward Eshu as he licked his lips. Eshu smiled. This was going to be too easy.

But then the pale Orisha stopped, lips slightly parted. "Wait. You took this from the Mortal Realm? You have shown yourself to one of them?"

"Nah..." Eshu replied. "I couldn't even if I attempted to. I'm just a whisper to mortal ears. Trust me, I've tried to communicate with them for centuries, just as you have."

"Oh... good, good." He turned away from Eshu—and the bottle—composing himself once more. "Shango has told me the same about the mortals' elevated skills in fermentation. *He* tried getting me to drink some as well." Despite his retreat, he kept giving the bottle sidelong glances over his shoulder. "What's the catch?"

Eshu drew back with an exaggerated hand to his chest. "No catch at all. I just want to see you do what you do best—what you were *made* to do, old friend."

Obatala stroked his chin, seeming to pull at the long beard that used to be there. He glanced at the changed image of his room, which still depicted his ceramic workshop.

Eshu was so close. His celestial comrade just needed some encouragement. A reminder of better times.

"I'm sure you recall when we used to drink near the Osun River. We used to play *ayoayo* as we watched the sun set in the Mortal Realm. Do you remember?"

Obatala chuckled inwardly. "Oh yes, I remember. Those were

simpler times. Before the Great Monarch set me to molding human bodies. And before Odu—" The Orisha was about to break his own rule by speaking the name. "Before I made a mess of everything."

"Let's have a bottle together. For old time's sake, at least."

The grimace on Obatala's face and his body drifting toward Eshu were at odds, each seemingly pulling against the other. "No, I cannot. I have too many responsibilities now. I can't be drinking."

"Fine, then. No drinking. But what about a game of ayoayo?"

Obatala took in another deep breath, then pierced Eshu with a stare of irritation. His first *true* glare of irritation. Eshu simply floated there with mirth, unfazed by the intense gaze.

"A game..." Obatala trailed, his expression softening. "A game I could do. You have been practicing since last time, I hope."

Eshu smiled. "You know it."

AND SO THE ORISHAS PLAYED THEIR GAME. THE RULES WERE simple: two rows of six holes filled with four cowries each. The objective was to "sow" more "seeds" than the opponent. First to twenty-one won.

The game was a simple one, but one of Eshu's favorites. On the surface, it was an elementary game for children, but in reality, it was a trickster's haven.

And Eshu loved setting his opponents up to make poor moves.

At that moment, however, he made sure to let Obatala win a few rounds. This was key. Of course, Eshu didn't let him win so many rounds—or so easily—that his ruse would be uncovered. Just enough to make Obatala think he had the edge. And for added distraction, Eshu peppered in some light chit-chat.

"You really gotta come down to the Mortal Realm with me sometime," he said after a particularly daring play. "They've got this thing called social media. Complete waste of time, but oh so fun."

"Oh yes." Obatala made his next move and smiled. "There's this one, erm, application the mortals keep dreaming about… it's called Insta-Spam? No. Insta-Lamb? No, that's not right. Insta-Yam? Something along those lines."

"Close enough." Eshu clutched his stomach. "Oh, some yams sound great right about now…"

Orisha couldn't eat food in the same way mortals could. Sure, they could pass meals across their mouths, but it was like tasting the ghost of something, not the full thing. One couldn't fully enjoy the flavor of mortal food unless one had a mortal body. That was something Eshu was looking forward to. He just needed to keep his wits about him, and a mortal body would be his.

As they got deeper and deeper into the game, floating in the middle of the chamber cross-legged, Eshu caught Obatala's gaze slipping to the palm wine, which hovered at their side. The trickster had deliberately taken swigs from it after each of his losses, smacking his lips so that the sweet tang could waft between them —and hopefully ensnare Obatala.

"How about we make this next game a bit more interesting?" Eshu finally asked. "If I win the following round, we will take a drink together. A little taste."

"And *when* I win," Obatala said, "What do I get then?"

Eshu stroked his chin. "*If* you win the next round… I'll lighten your load a little. I'll promise to come visit at least once every decade to help with your dreams. A thousand mortals for each of your victories. Directly, that is."

Obatala ran his hand over his bald head as though flipping back long strands of hair. "I would benefit from the help," he intoned. "Okay, Gatekeeper. You have a deal. But you've lost most of your games. Your victory seems… unlikely."

Not as unlikely as you think, Eshu thought, but what he said out loud was, "That's because I wasn't properly motivated before, old friend. On this next round, you had best come correct."

Obatala tilted his head. "Come correct?"

"Some more mortal-talk. Don't trip—I mean, don't worry yourself."

And so they continued their game, and Eshu handily won round after round. He had seen how Obatala played, recognized each of his moves and his preferred paths to victory. Eshu cut him off at every pass, winning every round by definitive leads. And with each of his victories, Obatala took a sip of the palm wine.

His first few were meager attempts at drinking, but with each loss, he took deeper and deeper swallows. Even on their seventh game, which he had surprisingly won, Obatala still took a drink—out of habit or because he was feeling himself, Eshu couldn't tell.

"All right, that's one-thousand of your mortals I'll overwatch," Eshu reminded him.

Obatala gave him an expression of mild confusion, then said, "Oh, right! Yes, yes."

By the twelfth round, and the twelfth chug of palm wine, Obatala had begun slurring his words.

That's when Eshu enacted his next gambit. "Okay, good games, good games. Now that you've loosened up, let's see if you've still got the touch." Eshu snapped his fingers, and a ceramic torso manifested between them. "I took the liberty of bringing this torso mold here from your workshop. Let's see what you can do with it. Complete it, if you can."

To Eshu's surprise, he was met without protest. Obatala, with the limp hands of one under the influence, started work on his mold. His hands stroked along the lumpy surface, turning it from something amorphous to the distinct figure of a human chest, human ribs, and human abs.

"Impeccable work, old friend." Eshu ran his hand over the outer layer of skin. It felt like the real thing, even down to the little hairs. "The belly is a little flabby, however."

Obatala shrugged. "I think it gives it a nice look... a unique shape."

Eshu wasn't about to get fussy about a little pudge, so he let it go. He couldn't talk anyway. He had a bit of a muffin top himself... Maybe that was Obatala's motivation. Plus, beggars couldn't be choosers, and this was more than he was hoping to achieve with Obatala in a single day. Skies, Eshu was expecting this whole ordeal to take at least a few years, maybe even a few decades.

His old friend must've been *really* lonely.

With Eshu's next win, Obatala gave the torso arms, and the win after that came the legs. All that remained after the third win was the most important piece, and the most difficult part.

Eshu snapped his fingers once more, and this time, the ayoayo board winked out of existence, replaced by a lumpy mold of an unfinished head.

"All right," Eshu said, "the last piece. You're almost there. If you can complete your work, I'll test drive it for you, take it down to the mortal realm and make sure it's well put together. What do you say? Make me a face that you think will suit me."

Obatala, now properly filled with the wine, wheezed and took up the challenge. Though the torso and limbs had only taken a few minutes, the head, and particularly the face, took several hours. Eshu, in patient silence, watched his old friend at work, and he couldn't have been prouder.

Lines cut through Obatala's forehead with the valleys of concentration, his lips pursed, his hands steady. Anytime he stopped to examine his work, he took another drink of the palm wine—Eshu assumed he did it to relax. Yet the measured way he moved his hands, the utter concentration in his slitted eyes, filled Eshu with joy.

And he hadn't even revealed the best part of the whole charade yet.

To pass the time, Eshu adjusted the dream room's prisms to show different landscapes with a flick of his finger like changing a human's television channel: an underwater cove with sharks that had glowing streaks along their heads, a swampy marsh with dark trees backdropped by vivid indigo, a volcanic vent smoldering molten rocks. Then he called forth several masks he had been working on. The other Orishas would've called his projects forgeries. Eshu preferred to call them homages.

He was in the middle of working out how to replicate the mask of Orunmila, the Orisha of Divination—and one of Obatala's neighbors—when the head was finally completed.

"You know something?" Obatala lifted the head aloft, turning it to see it in different angles of light. "It's not my best work... but I think it'll hold up."

Eshu floated across the room to examine the face. Not his best work, he said? It was *perfect.* Exactly what he needed: friendly, approachable, and most of all, unassuming.

"Do you mind?" Eshu nudged his chin to the completed body.

Obatala held out a steady hand. "By all means, Gatekeeper."

Eshu, taking in a deep breath, closed his eyes and concentrated.

He visualized himself as the body, forced his will through its bone, sinew, muscles, and skin alike. The longer he fixated on the human sensations of proper touch, proper scent, and proper sound, the weight of it all settled.

Being a human was both marvelous and exceedingly limiting.

He felt things he couldn't fully touch as an immortal. He expected human skin to feel clammy or moist with how much they sweated, but it was instead smooth and delicate. And the simple act of staying afloat amid the room took twice the effort than it had before, not only because the body was on the heavier side but because humans were filled with far less Ashe than the Orishas, which made them so light. Plus, Eshu had to keep reminding himself that he needed to actively breathe.

Then he opened his eyes.

My goodness, how blind the humans are, he thought.

It took several minutes for him to make out where he even was. The room's prisms, which had now returned to their default crystalline visage, blurred before him. The perfect clarity and field of view he was used to was cut in half. It was like being thrown into a dark tunnel with only the smallest morsel of light at the end.

His damned human eyes took their time, but eventually they cleared enough to make sense of the pale figure ahead. Where he expected to find the warm smile of Obatala, instead he was met with the countenance of sorrow.

"You know," Obatala said darkly, "This was the last body I started before I went into my drunken episode. The very last. I never thought I could do it again, could finish it..."

"But you have, old friend." Eshu placed his new hand on Obatala's shoulder. The effort felt slow and sluggish, and the Orisha's skin radiated with a heat Eshu wasn't expecting.

Despite Eshu's gesture of goodwill, Obatala still frowned. "My followers... what will they think of me? They know I don't drink. They know I abhor it. When the other Orishas find out, I'll never hear the end of it. I should never have taken a sip."

Eshu would have felt guilt at these words, but instead, he smiled. "Never fear. Your sobriety is still very much intact."

Obatala lifted his head; his eyebrow quirked. "What do you mean?"

"While true this was indeed palm wine," Eshu grabbed the bottle and poured it out, "it is *not* fermented, and thus, non-alcoholic."

Obatala's eyes descended with the liquid, which fell to the bottom of the room where, eventually, it splashed on the floor far, far below.

"You mean to say," he said, realization dawning on him, "*I* did all that myself."

"You did it all on your own, old friend."

Obatala stared at his hands, transfixed. For centuries, he must've thought he could never put them to work as they had been at the beginning of humankind. Now, he knew he could.

Eshu nodded his approval. He might've been a trickster, but that didn't make him heartless. With a small salute, he turned away from Obatala and drifted out of the room. He'd better get back to the Mortal Realm now. He could already feel his Orisha powers waning, and, with his new mortal body, he felt the need for a very long nap—a foreign concept to an Orisha.

"Where are you going?" Obatala called after him.

At the threshold of the dream room, Eshu waddled through a half turn and gave his old friend an awkward salute—it was going to take a while to get used to the human body. "I wasn't being dishonest when I said I'd test drive this body for you. There's someone I want to visit who needs a lesson of their own."

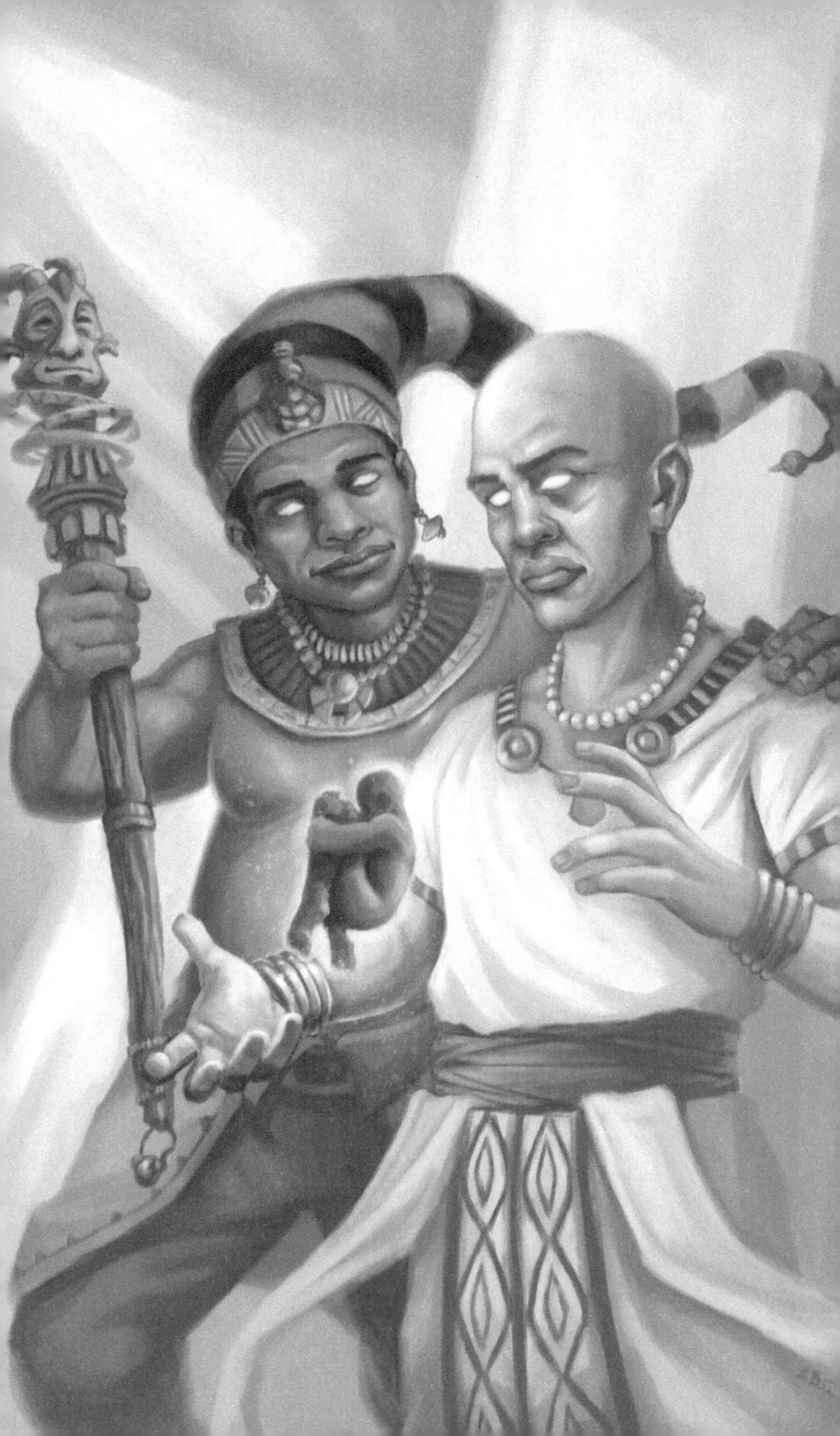

ANTOINE BANDELE

WHEN THE WIND SPEAKS

When the wind spoke, they used to listen.
When the wind spoke, their crowns would glisten.
Now the gusts fall on deaf ears
Gales whip for no one to hear
But She'll cut a path so clear
Listen, 'cause Oya is near...

- ELDER ADESINA ISOLA

WHEN THE WIND SPEAKS

Oya *didn't* have time.

She only had one shot at what she would attempt. The others would try to stop her if she tried to communicate with the girl. But it was a risk worth taking. And there were two reasons Oya would succeed:

One, she was no coward; two, she had Manuela Martinez.

This girl wasn't like Oya's other claimed children. Oya could speak through her other children subtly on the wind, but this particular girl was different. It was like a dam had broken when the mortal child had crossed over into the Orisha Plane two weeks ago with that TJ Young child, and Oya was the water who could finally run free to the other side.

The only issue now, however, was that the girl herself needed to realize it.

As the Saturday morning sun peeked over a Brooklyn row house, Oya heard the words she'd been waiting to hear the past fortnight through a lone window on the fifth floor:

"All right, *garatos*! Time for a Martinez boys' day out!"

Oya drifted along the A.M. breeze atop the currents that led her over the borough, through the streets, and straight into the cramp, narrow halls of the Martinez family apartment. Inside, a whirlwind of extended family—which could've rivaled even Oya's greatest storms—rushed about the modest kitchen where cousins, uncles, and fathers clamored for scrambled eggs, cassava, coffee, and juice.

Through the mass of faces ranging from light olive-tones to deep, dark umber, one might wonder if the household had any girls or mothers. But between the little boys looking to make away with the last coconut milk, or the older cousins who elbowed each other for the dwindling bacon, one could find three female faces that directed them all.

Well, at least they *tried* to direct them all.

"Michael, Luís, take two cups and split the milk!" Mrs. Martinez shouted, her voice hoarse from overuse.

"Gabriel, Adeyemo, y'all already had three pieces. Leave some bacon for your father," cried her cousin, *Tia* Terresa, whose bags hung heavy under shadowed lids.

But of most concern to Oya that day was the youngest of the women, a young lady with a lion's mane of curly hair who dashed between coffee pot, skillet, and oven like she was on some competition show for top chefs.

"Elijah, I told you to get those eggs cracked and whisked for me," she huffed. "And Benny, you shouldn't be fightin' over no bacon when your little butt 'posed to be at the store getting more orange juice."

"Okay, okay, Miss Bossy, gimme a minute," Benny answered. "And who you callin' little? I'm one year younger than you and two inches taller."

"Fine. Then deal with these eggs and I'll go to the store."

Benny got real quiet then, and no protest came from his lips as he grabbed a thin tank top and headed out. It was only morning, yet the heat of another hot summer's day already stuck to the row house's brick walls.

These boys finna make me go upside one of their heads, Oya heard Manny thinking as the young woman wiped sweat from her bushy brows.

Oya knew Manny had been looking forward to that day. She only needed to suffer her brothers and cousins for one hour more and then they'd be gone for the *entire* weekend to the Beaver Pond Campground, leaving the trio of ladies of the house alone for some much needed rest.

Ever since Manny got back from Camp Olosa, home life had been hectic. Without letting her know, her parents had decided to invite her cousins to their already cramped three-bedroom apartment, where sharing space—notably Manny's own room—was more than a challenge among the seven cousins added to her four brothers. It was bad enough she was outnumbered on the daily, now she didn't even try to keep up.

But as the "tornado of toddlers" settled down and started to file out into two rented vans, Oya could hear Manny's mind quiet for the first time in two weeks.

And it was about damn time.

There was a message the girl needed to hear.

When Manny was younger, Oya had an easier time communicating with her. There were even times Oya could show her face to her divine child through imaginary friends, her toys, even within the wind itself. Now, like with all of her chosen children, it was like Oya was attempting conversations with drywalls.

If there wasn't a mini-family reunion occupying Manny's headspace, it was her muddled feelings about her old friend at Ifa, or her new friend at Camp Olosa, or the summer job she didn't take when she could've helped *Mamãe* and *Papai* with the rent. At that moment, however, despite having a distinctly quiet room all to herself, a single email weighed heavy on her mind.

Oya watched from the corners of the room as the flashing light of her cellphone winked in and out across Manny's bit lip. The pulling of her phone, the unlocking of her screen, and the tapping of her email app had become a habit at that point, even if the child hadn't realized it yet. Anytime she had any semblance of free time, this had become her routine.

"Manuela Morayo Martinez, you have been accepted to Ifa Academy of Tomorrow's Diviners," she read quietly to herself. "With permission from your parent or guardians' signature, please return a reply no later than the twenty-eighth of August."

Manny scrolled to her calendar app, which at that moment read "August 27th." She scrolled back to her email app and her thumb made its practiced tap of the trash icon, forcing the email into a "deleted" folder for all of a few minutes before she went back into it, restored the email as "unread" then started the process anew.

Read. Delete. Restore. Read. Delete. Restore.

Oya had to put a stop to it. This was not the time for one of her divine children to spiral into her usual cycle of overthinking. She needed to have a clear head; she needed to be receptive to Oya's call.

Pushing herself from the corners of the room, Oya focused on the chipped window that was left slightly ajar. And with a little celestial shimmy, Oya danced around the sliver of the open window, causing it to whistle.

What Manny did next would determine if Oya could really get through to her, and as the young teen edged her chin to the gust squeezing its way into her room, Oya grew excited. With the hot day, the breeze should've been a welcome one...

But Oya's hopes had been dashed before.

For the past few weeks, whenever Oya crafted her little trills on the wind, Manny had always closed the window instead of opening it wide as she so often did in the past.

Swinging her legs over her bed, Manny shuffled to her window. Oya caught the small movement of her hands, which reached for the top of the window sill instead of the bottom.

No, no, no, not this time, Oya thought earnestly.

As Manny drew the window down, Oya shot a spellwind into a coin jar, forcing a bronze coin to implant itself at the window sill where Manny couldn't fully close it. Manny tugged at the window a few times before realizing what had stopped it.

Oh, shit, what are the odds of that happening? she thought as she pulled at the coin to free it.

What were *the odds?* Oya thought back, agitated.

The odds were astronomical! The coin was upright for crying out loud, perfectly balanced. And how had Manny not noticed it was the very unique Oya coin her aunt had given her that summer. The sign should've been clear who was vying for her attention.

They couldn't keep playing this game, she and Manny. Now that Oya was making a direct play to communicate to a mortal, one of the Orishas would be on her tail soon.

There had to be something else Oya could do... but what?

Taking notice of the spiralling rainbow rug under Manny's bed, Oya knew exactly what needed to be done. Just as Manny got the coin free, Oya breathed one last gale through the window slit, causing the coin jar to fall over and onto the rug.

"Woah!" Manny let out in a sharp breath.

A collection of pennies, nickels, dimes, quarters, and most importantly, Oya coins, spread wide along the multi-colored rug. To any normal mortal, the spread would've appeared as nothing more than a haphazard assortment of coppers, silvers, and gold, but to a diviner practicing under the Orishas, it should've been a clear message.

Between the spirals of *burgundy and purple*, Oya made sure to lay out *nine* of her coins along their edges. There was no way Manny wouldn't notice; Oya was practically shouting her presence in the room. Those were her holy colors and that was her ordained number, respectively.

"Manny, you klutz," she mumbled under her breath. She made the move to clean up but stopped suddenly as her fingers traced over the Oya coins. "Wait a minute..." Her hand trembled slightly. "Nah, no way. It can't be."

Yes! There it is. See it, my child.

The slow turn of Manny's head, her wandering eyes trailing the edges of the room, nearly made Oya kick up a hurricane just outside the rowhouse.

And then... Manny's phone *buzzed-buzzed.*

It always had to be her wretched phone!

Oya had battled many great forces during her very long existence, overwatched countless wars, yet she had never met a pair of enemies so fearsome, so painstakingly relentless as Father Technology and Mother Internet.

As though she had never seen the coins at all, Manny went straight for her phone to check her notifications. The buzzing had been a notification for a promotion for an old video store going out of business near Hell's Kitchen. That wouldn't have been so bad on its own if it wasn't for the slew of other red dots, pop-ups, and dings her phone seemingly decided to throw at Manny at the very same moment Oya had been contending for her attention. One measly notification led to another, and another, and eventually Manny found herself in a text message thread with one of her friends.

Only Olodumare could know when *that* conversation would end.

And with the window now closed, Oya had no means to pull Manny away.

But Oya would be damned if her husband Shango came hounding her about direct influence over mortals. She *knew* it was forbidden. She *knew* she shouldn't be doing what she was doing. But she didn't care. Have all the Orishas come after her and see what they could do against her hurricanes.

Not like it mattered though. Social media did all the heavy lifting to halt her.

Manny was already gathering the coins back in her jar as she mindlessly tapped away at her phone. If only she had still been back at camp where the mortal diviners didn't allow their children to have any devices with them. Oya would've had a much easier time then.

Manny grabbed a purple sweater she tied around her waist and headed out. Oya followed her through the cramped halls, as each of Manny's steps squeaked along old wooden flooring.

"Hey, Mamãe," Manny said as she entered the living room where Mom and Tia Terresa were soaking their feet in warm bowls of water. "Niko's Video is going out of business. I wanted to stop by and see how he's doing. Can I go?"

Tia snorted with surprise. "That *velhote* is still in business? The gentrification over there didn't swallow him up yet?"

"You know how stubborn Mr. B is," Mom answered lazily. "And yes, amor. Just be back before six."

Manny gave Mom a peck on the cheek. An open window with long curtains sat just behind the sofa Mom sat on—the perfect opportunity for Oya. With another push of her *Ashe,* she ran her winds along the linen. Manny seemed to notice, drawing her gaze along the curtain with curious eyes.

"Oh, that breeze is so needed right now," Tia Terresa sighed soothingly. "Manny, let me brush your hair before you go. You look so wild. Shoot, maybe we should put a hot comb through it too."

"Ah, Tee Tee, you know that's the look these days." Mom turned to Manny. "*Você está linda, bebê.*"

Manny had no trouble ignoring Tia's comments—her remarks were often bordering on rude but everyone in the family just got used to it. Leaning down to give Tia a kiss too, Manny said with a smile, "Don't worry, Tia, I can hook you up with a perm real quick. I got some enchanted curlers in the bathroom right now."

Tia Terresa flipped her long, straight hair over her shoulder. "I think I'm good. Oh! And don't forget to give Jessica a kiss before you leave, amor."

Manny didn't need reminding of that. She never left or came into the house without paying respects to her late cousin. Instead of giving Tia sass she answered, "Of course, Tia. You and Mamãe be good until I get back, you hear?"

"We're always good." Mom winked as Manny made for the family altar. She kissed two of her fingers, set them along a picture of her cousin, mumbled a little prayer then headed for the door. As Oya followed, a rush ran through her after Manny's prayer and she made sure it travelled safely on her winds to Cousin Jessie's spirit. Manny muttered a second prayer at the door, a message to Eshu the Gatekeeper to bless her with a safe journey, reminding Oya of her timeline. But upon a second thought, Oya wondered if no other Orisha would come after her or try to stop her. After all, the mortals had all sorts of reports and rumors about other Orisha showing themselves to them. Perhaps there was some leeway being given, or maybe whatever Manny and her friends did in the Aqua Realm had triggered something, some undetectable bond between mortal and deity.

It was all the more reason Oya needed to warn Manny about Olokun, all the more reason Oya needed Manny to get a very important message to TJ Young.

Despite not having any other Orishas hounding her, Oya still had to contend with not only social media and flashing notifications on Manny's phone, but with Brooklyn and New York city itself. Manny had decided to take the C-Line to Hell's Kitchen, and she didn't notice any of Oya's signs.

When Oya roiled a little cyclone of newspapers near the subway to grab her attention, Manny swatted them away, which made her knock someone's drink out of their hand—thankfully it was only water. Then on the subway when Manny was gazing out the window, Oya altered the thermals in the sky so that a set of seagulls would fly in the shape of her holy symbol, but Manny was too busy staring out at the billboards passing by about new TV shows coming to several streaming services. And when Manny got out of the subway near Times Square to buy a hotdog for old man Niko, Oya forced the burgundy and purple flags on a the vendor's corner stand to flit in the air—while all the other flags remained still, yet Manny was too distracted by a jolly street performer dressed as a clown with a muffin top and a red-and-black scepter in hand. Oya did a double take at the sign next to the clown which read: *Will work for yams*.

It wasn't until Manny stepped away from the loud distractions of Times Square to the more muted ambiance of Hell's Kitchen—well, muted in the sense that there was only taxi honking instead of everything else—that Oya thought she could show her presence unabated. Making the banners along Niko's Video hop along a gentle wind current, Oya attempted to replicate the music of a whispering tree, something Manny had always been attuned to. For a moment it seemed as though Manny took notice of the fluttering as a smile curled at her cheek, but the smirk was born from her phone once again, not Oya's presence.

What's she distracted by now, Oya thought.

Twisting for a better view, Oya drifted over Manny's shoulder to spy. On the child's screen was what the mortals called a "text message thread."

MANNY

U know u're way funnier over text

MANNY

Ur GIF choices are...

The child sent off a little animated picture of a chef kissing his hand and throwing it to the air.

MANNY

btw have u ever seen dusk of the blood moon b4?

TJ

thats not that 🧛🐺 stuffz is it?

MANNY

yup yup im gonna buy some copies for us right now 😊 they'll be waiting for you in brookyln

TJ! Oya thought. The *TJ Young!?*

Oya needed to get Manny's attention then and there. She kicked up the winds under the banners but that did nothing. And before she could whistle a song atop the wind, Manny opened the door to Niko's Video, a ding signalling her entrance.

The small store was packed with people shoulder to shoulder, some wearing weird combinations of clothing and lots of flannel, wide-brimmed hats, twisted mustaches on the men and brightly dyed hair on the women. Half the shelves lined to the right were completely empty. The section to the left was one long line of registers, yet only one man protected the station. No, not protected. It only *seemed* he was protecting his area from the mass of people asking prices for limited edition DVDs of this and signed posters of that. Behind the hurried-looking man with the short-cropped hair and stubbled beard, a moving picture of knights on horses charged forward with war cries, each of them trapped in rows and columns of square boxes called "televisions."

Oya knew Niko's Video was Manny's favorite, though Oya didn't know why. The place smelled of a funky odor, the single room was dimly lit, and there was a family of rats that made their home near the back corner between an wrinkled cardboard cut out of the Terminator and an old gumball machine. Perhaps Manny favored it because the hole in the wall was a far cry from Times Square or Coney Island, just a little nook that tourists hardly ever visited.

Well, except *that* day, it seemed.

"Hey, li'l Manuela!" the thick-browed cashier croaked out. That had to be Niko of Niko's Video. "Here to see me off? I haven't seen the store this busy since your ma and pa were your age."

"I had to bring you one last hot dog!" Manny beamed. "Chili, no mustard, and extra ketchup."

"Manuela, you're an angel!" Niko was perhaps the only person in the world who was allowed to call Manny by her full name, except members of her family, of course. Manny never had the heart to correct him, or rather, as Oya knew, Manny enjoyed the fact that Niko kept all new releases just for her, so she didn't want to risk losing that. Mom still couldn't let go of her DVDs despite all the streaming services out there, and Niko was one of the few Mom and Pops that still sold them.

"*Always support local*," Mom had always said.

"Take whatever you want from the bargain bin." Niko nodded to the rusty old cart near a stand selling microwave popcorn.

"I got money today. I'll pay." Manny waved the freebie away. "You still have *Dusk of the Blood Moon*?"

Niko pulled out a DVD box from behind his sticker-filled countertop. "I had a feeling I'd see you today. The latest came in on Wednesday." He winked and handed the box to her.

Manny gave him a few bills of cash. "Sorry about the shop, Mr. Niko."

"Don't worry yourself. This just forces me to retire like you always said I should."

Enough chit-chat, Oya thought as another thrift-shop-fashioned couple walked through the door with a ding. A glint caught Oya's attention, a reflection off a Spider-Man action figure propped next to a remote control along the man's countertop.

That's it!

Using the slight gust traveling through the door, Oya forced the action figure on its side where it landed on the remote control to change the channel. There had to be something on that would grab Manny's attention. A sports game. An old movie. A music video. A cooking show—wait!

Using the last morsel of wind still hanging in the store, Oya forced Spider-Man to change the channel back to a music video that played a song, an old Spanish song by someone named Julio Iglesias... a song named "Manuela".

Manny looked up curiously at the television sets lining the back of the shop, each of them showing a tan-looking man on a stage like the eyes of an insect.

Niko glanced over his shoulder after checking out his latest customer. "Now what you look at this. What a coincidence that is. Eh, Manuela?"

There you go, child. Listen to the words, Oya thought eagerly.

But just as the singer was about to belt his chorus—which was a repeat of the name "Manuela," somehow the TV screen changed to a cartoon monkey speaking to a cartoon lion that said, "Nope. Wrong again! Ha ha hah!" And of course, Manny shook the curiosity from her head and turned her attention elsewhere.

Niko banged one of the old TV sets and grunted, "I don't know what's going with these things. They just started acting up now."

Oya would've tried something else to grab Manny's attention, but something about that cartoon monkey—who apparently was named Rafiki—seemed oddly familiar to her. Was it the voice, the way the monkey bounced around like a jovial buffoon, or something else entirely...

"I'll take all of these," Manny said, breaking Oya from her stupor. The young woman carried a box that read "Dusk of the Blood Moon: The Complete Collection."

"You mind taking the rest of the store with you too?" Niko laughed.

"Don't trip, Mr. B. All these hipsters will beat me to it." Manny's phone chimed in her pocket. She answered it. "Hey, Ma. Huh? What? Yeah... yeah. I can get that for you." She dropped her phone and lifted her voice to Niko. "The farmer's market is open today right?"

"Yeah, just down 57th. Walking distance."

"Yeah, Ma. I'm right around the corner. I'll grab the stuff and be back real soon." Manny mouthed a silent "thank you" to Niko and stepped out of the shop.

THAT STRANGE CARTOON MONKEY WAS STILL ON OYA'S MIND as she followed Manny to the 57th Street Greenmarket. The high-pitched voice still weighed on her mind, even as Manny picked up everything Mamãe asked for. Oya had nearly forgotten what she was doing there in the first place until Manny passed by a row of eggplants.

Nothing else had worked but maybe that would...

After all, eggplants were Oya's favorite.

With another brush of wind coming down through the narrow high rises of old brick and mortars, Oya made the eggplants do a little dance. Nothing so crazy that would warrant unwanted attention, mortal and immortal alike, but just enough so that if Manny saw them, she'd take a second look and connect the dots.

But just like all the other times that day, Manny took a small notice and something got in the way. This time it was Manny's own unlaced shoe laces she tripped over. What was going on? This couldn't just be a series of bad luck scenarios...

Nothing seemed to work. Desperation taking hold, there was only one other thing Oya could think to do but it would surely garner the attention of the other Orishas. She'd heard rumors of the others who tried to reveal themselves directly to the mortals, how the other Orishas were trapped in some powerful staff as punishment. But rumors ran wild in the Orisha Plane, and Oya, for lack of a better phrase, had to throw caution to the winds.

Manny gathered her fruit and veggies in a bag, then turned down the corner to a bank with tall windows. Oya gathered her Ashe within her and implanted it to the reflection. Manny halted her casual gait almost at once, dropping her fruits and veggies on the sidewalk.

The gape of her jaw was unmistakeable.

"Oya?" she asked to what must've looked like nothing to the rest of the passerby.

Oya tried to respond but she knew her words would only come as a whisper to the mortal, no more than a jumbled murmur like the drone of wind.

"Oya?" Manny asked again. "Is that... I didn't believe the rumors—I mean, I should've—this summer's been mad crazy." She touched the bank window. "Why can't you speak?"

Oya gestured to the street performer who sang a song titled "I'm Coming Home."

Manny quirked an eyebrow. "Home? Are you saying I should go home? What should I do there?"

Oya blew her winds in the direction of a vendor selling sage. Manny gasped. "The family altar? Can I speak to you there?"

Oya nodded, smiling. But she inclined her head toward a clock over the bank. Oya knew her image would only last so long. She could already feel herself waning.

"Not much time? I think I understand." Manny pulled out her phone and jogged off down the street. "I'll get a rideshare back home. Damn, where's TJ when you need him?"

"Excuse me, young lady!" An elderly voice called from behind, holding up the fallen fruits and veggies. "You've dropped something."

Jogging, Manny called out over her shoulder, "Sorry, can you take it! I gotta be somewhere real quick!"

New York traffic was maddening. A huddle of cars without end. Manny's active thoughts raced with question after question.

What does Oya want?

Did something happen with Olokun like TJ said?

Are we in danger?

Oya desperately wanted to answer her child, and she would

the moment they made the connection at her home altar. There were enough homages to Oya on the dresser to at least get a short message out. There, Oya could explain the unique connection between them, how TJ could stop Olokun before he wreaked havoc on the mortals.

But they didn't have time for this... this endless line of steel and rubber. Oya preferred it when the mortals had used horses, or better yet, their own two feet. At any moment, one of the other Orishas would show up and put a stop to all this.

Oya couldn't tell who was more nervous, her or Manny, who kept looking over to the car window Oya had implanted herself in.

"I never would have thought you'd look like that," Manny said to the window. "You're beautiful but... fierce."

Oya wanted to say "just like you, child," but her voice was still devoid of weight.

"What's that?" Manny's driver asked up front.

Manny's back straightened. "Oh, nothing. I was just saying there's so much traffic."

"Sorry, I'm getting all the red lights right now."

Oya waved in Manny's direction, then pointed down an alley.

"What about down here," the girl said. "I can get you extra. I gotta be home real fast."

"How much we talkin'?"

"Uh... Ten?"

The driver rolled his eyes. "Thirty."

"C'mon, I'm already payin' extra in the app..."

"Thirty."

Manny sighed. "Twenty."

"Deal."

Oya directed Manny down shortcut after shortcut, but every time progress was made they seemed to have to double back because of some new traffic jam or construction work that Oya would've sworn wasn't there before. For every step forward they took two back, it seemed.

Then it hit Oya. There was a reason no Orisha had yet come after her.

Because there had been one with her the entire day.

The clown who distracted Manny at Times Square with his red-and-black scepter, the cartoon monkey at the video store, the traffic lights that seemed to put them in a perpetual circle. It was a miraculous misadventure of mischief. The work of only one certain Orisha.

And here she was leaving hints for her claimed child when there was someone else trying to capture *her* attention.

"Damnit, Eshu... is that you?" Oya sighed. "I was wondering why no one was interfering with me."

Eshu revealed himself at the adjacent window from Oya. He looked just as jolly as ever, wide smile and big eyes almost mocking Oya before he said, "Hey, Manny. How's it going?"

But the girl didn't respond, looking straight *through* Eshu's image to the pedestrians on the sidewalks.

"Oh, can she not see me? Why can she see you, Windweaver?"

"Because she's *my* claim, *my* child. Not yours, Gatekeeper. Whatever you did with that boy triggered something between her and me. This wouldn't be working otherwise. Besides, I'm having a hard enough time having her see me even now."

Eshu shrugged. "Oh well... Any whoozle, you know how many rules you had me break today? I *know* you're not trying to consult with the Mortal Realm without first asking me, old friend. I tried to give you the benefit of the doubt, to give you a chance. I know you heard rumors of what happened to Olosa when she tried to go over my head..."

"Yes. And I also know she evaded you for years."

"Ugh, do not remind me."

Oya wondered why Eshu didn't outright stop her from the start. The Gatekeeper worked in mysterious ways, but one thing was clear with him when it came to going over his head... you don't do it. Ever.

"What is your plan here? Nothing good will come from speaking with the girl."

"Olokun needs to be put back in chains. You know that. The girl can get me in touch with that TJ boy. I hear he's some sort of an... amplifying conduit to Ashe."

"The boy isn't *that* powerful. Trust me. We did our best and we didn't make a dent when we faced Olokun."

Manny glanced up at Oya again as they came to a stop at yet another red light. Oya gave her a coy smile, engaging with Eshu again only when the girl looked back up front. "I'm going to ask for Shango's help, of course."

"Aren't you two on a break right now? Last time I heard he was trying to take your head."

"That was centuries ago. And he'll get over it if it means a good fight with Olokun."

Eshu *tsked tsked*. "No matter. I tried to give you hints all day, Windweaver. You did not come through me. I have to put a stop to this. Olokun made a deal with the boy and you can't go interfering with that. Go speak to the Dreamweaver, he can help you the *right* way with your divine child."

"Olokun broke all that when he trapped Olosa in your staff."

"Then... you give me no choice, old friend."

CRASH!

Several cars ahead of them in a wide intersection, at least a dozen cars slammed into each other, bringing the already slow-moving traffic to an utter stand still. Worst yet, the intersection had to be Times Square itself.

They were trapped.

"It's better this way, Oya." Eshu waved and winked out of existence from the adjacent window. Yet his voice remained. "You'll thank me later; they always do!"

The damned Trickster. He knew Oya's time with Manny was limited. And the crash all but put a stake into any chance of communication.

"Got anymore of those little shortcuts?" The driver asked

jokingly. Manny turned to Oya; Oya shook her head. "Don't worry 'bout it. We'll sit through this and get those shortcuts going again."

"How long you think we'll have to wait?" Manny asked.

The driver peeked at the time on his app. "Knowing New York city emergency services... it'll be a little while, if I'm honest."

Oya grabbed Manny's attention again and shook her head. That wouldn't be enough time. Their connection would sever in mere moments.

"I'm going to get out right here. You can still head to Brooklyn so you get paid. Here, thanks for trying." Manny tossed him two ten-dollar bills. "The subway is just off 42nd, right?"

"Yeah, just up this way. Good luck, kid."

"Thanks."

Manny hopped out of the car and slipped between bikers, carts, and tourists trying to get a better look of the wreck. Shouldering through the crowd, Manny slipped into the bustling Times Square with all its lit-up billboards, shouting mobs, and more than interesting aromas. It would've been an impossible task on a normal day, but Oya opened path after path for Manny, nudging one shawarma stand aside or groups of tourists that huddled too closely. It was the least she could do, but it was a desperate effort.

In less than a minute, Manny made it to the stairs leading down to the subway, but only to be met with a sea of people spilling up and over into the streets. They bumped into Manny's shoulders, shoved their way up to a street that already lacked in real estate for their feet to stand on.

"What's going on?" Manny asked Oya.

It was one of the subway workers who answered. "All the subways in Manhattan are shut down until further notice."

"What!? All of Manhattan? How? I have to get to Brooklyn *right now*, yo."

"Young lady, please calm down. We are working to get the trains back up as soon as we can."

Oya felt Manny's rage as though it were her own, that

warrior's fire all her children possessed. The child lifted her eyes to the window of a nearby restaurant. Rushing over, she pounded the window. "No, no! Oya, you're disappearing. What do I do? Tell me what to do!?"

But Oya couldn't do anything. All she could do was bellow shouts that were blocked from Mortal Realm. Her rage must've been written on her manifested face, because Manny called out, "Oya, what's wrong? Are you hurt? What's happening?"

"Young lady, young lady," the subway worker said, pulling at Manny's arms. "Are you okay?"

A tourist nearby murmured. "Is she... crazy?"

"You know how New York is," replied her partner.

"I'm not crazy!" Manny shouted back and stomped her way through Times Square aimlessly. Oya knew she was looking for guidance, searching for anything that could help their connection point. But one mortal child wouldn't be enough to bring Oya back to the Mortal Realm, no matter how much she believed on her own.

Feeling herself fade back into her natural winds once more, Oya gathered more Ashe within herself.

"Don't do it," she heard Eshu called out in her head. "Don't force my hand, Oya."

Oya ignored him, amassing more and more Ashe into one concentrated effort. Then, when she was nearly too full, as storm clouds rushed around the Manhattan skyline, as Manny cried out despite the side-eyes she received from onlookers, Oya dived into Manny's spirit.

And she and Manny were one.

"No, Oya! No!" Eshu exclaimed.

But the Gatekeeper was too late. The power had manifested, and there was nothing that could stop the maelstrom that was Oya and Manny's combined strength as Manny lifted off her feet in the middle of the busiest intersection of the United States. Wind whistled around them both, gusts cast from Manny's fingers, and a cyclone spread out around her, smashing into every storefront, every colorful billboard, every local and tourist alike.

Glass shattered. Car horns blared. And mortals screamed for their lives.

All the lights went out, leaving Times Square blanketed in the dying sun's amber hue.

Then, suddenly, Oya felt herself being pulled from Manny's body, could see herself being transformed into a purple and burgundy mist.

"I didn't want to have to do this, Windweaver," Eshu sighed gravely. He had not manifested in the Mortal Realm, but instead was pulling Oya back to the Orisha Plane. No, not just back to the Orisha Plane, but into the staff she had heard rumor of: the Gatekeeper's staff.

"Manny, can you hear me?" Oya called out as she was ripped away from reality.

"Yes, Oya! I can hear you. I can hear you."

"Find my husband; summon Shango. Get TJ to Sky Realm. You must train more. Olokun must be stopped. Eshu has me in his —" Oya's voice cut off, her mouth sucked into Eshu's staff.

"I will, Oya! I'll tell him!"

Oya's final moment seemed to hang in the air for a brief eternity as she receded back into Eshu's staff. Manny hung in the air over clusters of gawking people, between the dim light, among still air.

And then she fell.

But at least the message was conveyed...

Oya just had to hope it was enough to save the mortals.

ANTOINE BANDELE

AN AXE FOR A HAMMER

War demands sacrifices,
not only from the soldiers who fight,
but from the hearts that await their return...

- UNKNOWN

1

The Court of All was a perfect stage for Oshosi. The Orisha of Justice and the Hunt was going to make one for the history books, even among the Gods. Like spotlights to a thespian, the lights cutting through the grandiose gilded windows haloed Oshosi. Stars and gas clouds served as a backdrop to the seamless glass panes. A set of public benches, sheeted in opulent copper, supplied seating for a rainbow of ethereal creatures. But they were not Oshosi's primary audience. His back was turned to the crowd, his attention fixed ahead on the grand golden stand where the ultimate arbiters of justice sat in wait. A hodgepodge sampling of every pantheon from the almost forgotten Mortal Realm:

From Ma'at of Ancient Egypt with a feather in her hair and wings at her back, to Inanna of Old Mesopotamia, appearing almost like the former's twin with her wings, though her head was topped with horns. And of course Themis, with her blindfold over her eyes and scales under her palm, serving as their head—front and center.

In total, seven deities sat behind their audacious golden stand, listening earnestly to the testimony Oshosi was giving. From what Shango could see, chained and bound to his defense chair, none of them seemed in any way pleased.

In fact, each deity wore various forms of frowns, pinched lips, and subtle scowls. Could Shango blame them when he was being tried for the death of the Mighty Thor? No, not just the mighty...

His friend.

His brother.

Of all the testy deities, none were angrier than Thor's sons, Magni and Modi, who sat at the prosecution table with curled fists and narrowed brows. Magni, his hair cascading like molten gold, sat tall and strong, his stormy eyes crackling with the power of thunder. Modi imitated his older brother's posture and expression, but he had tied his fiery reddish-blond hair in a messy bun.

Shango did his best not to let his gaze drift to them for too long, shame swelling in his heart.

"I don't have to convince them all," Oshosi had told Shango before the court case had begun. "Just the majority," he added with a wink and a cheeky grin. "Worst case: we'll get you off on a deadlock. That'll give me more time to establish a better defense. Or... we can use the Fates and Anansi as I suggested before. It would make this whole thing a lot easier."

"No," Shango had told him sharply. "No, we will not."

The Fate and War deities were always at odds because of their differing approaches to fighting the shadows in their never-ending war. The Fates, shrouded in their enigmatic ways, employed methods that confound the comprehension of the War Gods, making their strategies and interventions all but inscrutable. This fundamental disparity had kept the relationship between these two ethereal factions fraught with tension. The War Gods relentlessly pushed the boundaries of destiny, often triggering repercussions from the Fates. The latest—and perhaps most grievous—transgression in this ongoing power struggle had been the tragic demise of Thor.

Shango had no interest in applying more flame to that burning bridge between the two forces. Deep down, part of him wanted to believe Thor didn't die for nothing, that the Fates truly had a good reason for allowing him to meet his end.

"Just..." Shango had said softly to Oshosi. "Just get me off without bringing Anansi and the Fates into this. Find another way."

"That's a tall order, old friend," Oshosi had started to say, but changed his tune after Shango gave him a scowl. "But... I'll see what I can do."

In the present, Oshosi spoke with his hands. A lot.

That's what annoyed Shango the most.

Shango still wasn't used to how much the Orisha—a former comrade—had changed. Oshosi used to mete out Jungle Justice, not Joker Justice. In times past, he was more likely to cast the accused to the bush and have Mother Nature be their ultimate judge. But he had stayed behind on the Mortal Realm as an over-watcher, like most of the Orishas after the Great Separation.

Eshu the Trickster had been a bad influence on him, apparently.

Shango decided not to think about it too much. Oshosi's theatrics within the grand courtroom were just a buzzing in his ear. The empty seats to either side of the Justice Council were what dominated Shango's thoughts. When the Great War had started in eons past, there were at least two or three dozen council members representing the humans of every corner of the Mortal Realm. Now they were down to seven.

When had the war even started? Shango thought. *When had so many deities fallen to it?*

An image conjured in Shango's mind: long, flowing golden hair that stretched to a full beard. Strong arms, and stronger hands wielding a great hammer.

Remember your heart, brother, Thor said in Shango's mind. *Never forget it.*

It almost sounded real. Shango wanted it to be.

Shango edged his chin over his shoulder to give his wife, Oya, a sad smile. She sat among the audience on the public benches. Despite the mess Shango created, she remained regal and stoic in her customary burgundy wrappings. She and Shango had bought the mortals of their ancient domain a little time, helped win the fight for the human's coastal home against their old adversary, Olokun. But it was at the cost of the closest friend Shango had ever had.

So... was it worth it? Shango thought. It didn't feel like it. The real fight was out here, among the cosmos, against the true enemy.

As Oshosi went over primordial laws and proper adjudication with the council, Shango edged his eyes to one of the tall windows that backdropped the Council. It peered out into an endless hellscape of gas clouds and interstellar galaxies, older than the deities of the Mortal Realm themselves. A window to the greater battle from the safety of a court that couldn't possibly appreciate the sacrifices of war.

Shango frowned. Every so often, a star would wink out or a shadow would envelop a trail of fog: the signs of a battle waged and a battle lost to those dreadful, dark entities.

The God Eaters.

Another star died in the distant darkness, and Shango suppressed a scowl that wasn't prudent for a court setting.

To keep his eyes from witnessing any more stars getting snuffed out, he stared down at his shackled arms. His gaze fell over a pale streak that extended from wrist to bicep. It was a battle wound earned long ago. The first time he met the Mighty Thor.

2

SEVERAL EONS AGO, THE DAY THE ORISHAS JOINED IN THE Great Separation between the Mortal and Ethereal Realms, Shango was one of the first to leave. He had told his fellows it was to fight the Great War, to honor his kin as one of the most powerful among their pantheon. Privately, though, he was only seeking a challenge he could no longer find on Earth.

He had been the one to secure the Oyo Empire beneath his thumb after years of turmoil. He had uncovered the sacred pot that had graced him with the power of lightning. And he had been the one chiefly responsible for imprisoning the great Olokun in the Orisha's underwater fortress.

With nothing more to challenge him, it made sense for him to pack his axes and enlist.

Many of the pantheons went to a place called the End Realm, which the Asgardians and Yoruba called *Utenheim* and *Ijọba Ipari* respectively. It was a space initially designed by the Asgardians and built in concert with all the other deity groups. To protect the Mortal Realm from the dangers of the God Eaters, they crafted a dimension that rested outside of space and time. And this domain housed the Great War, housed Shango and all the others that took up the mantle of holding the horrors at bay.

In those first few days, the camp of the Bolt Battalion reverberated with not only the song of blades but with the chime of magic. Sparring sessions between ethereal beings exploded across an asteroid among the stars. Atop the rocky surface, several tents of different cultures clashed in endless rows. Pixies, giants, and amorphous creatures from every pantheon tested their mettle against one another.

Submerged under a cloak of sweat, Shango pressed an attack against the curly-bearded Marduk. The god had called himself a Master of Lightning. While he proved a moderate challenge for Shango, he must've been well past his prime. Marduk's bolts were powerful, but they were far too sluggish for Shango's twin axes. Nearly as soon as their sparring match had begun, Marduk held out his arms to yield.

"Hah!" Zeus roared with mirth from his floating marble throne as he slapped his knee with a fist. He gripped his famed thunderbolt between meaty fingers. The smacking of his knee caused bolts to spark harmlessly between his palms, and rolling thunder tore through the heavens. The sound somehow surpassed his laughter. His throne floated above the sparring asteroid of the camp, his drooping white robes rolling over the side as he said, "Shango, Shango, Shango. I've not seen bolts so sharp and swift in quite some time. Why have I not heard of you and your power?"

Marduk, chin cast to the ground where his curly beard swayed, spoke. "Forgive my defeat, High General Zeus. If this were but a few millennia ago—when my people worshiped me as they once did—I would be in better condition."

Zeus surveyed the camp. At its center was a ring made of giants' bones that bordered a pit a few dozen yards deep. There had been a small audience that day. Only a score of the gods were assessing the new recruits from the Mortal Realm. That and a half dozen deities of desire that wrapped themselves around Zeus' limbs: Female, male, and everything in between.

"Do not fret, old friend," Zeus said. "We shall find a place for you in the vanguard."

"You honor me, High General." Marduk bowed and climbed his way out of the pit. Then, in shame, he shouldered his way between the shimmering armor of the observing group.

Zeus stroked his curly white hair as he assessed Shango once more. "You may well be a challenge even for me, Hero. But there is another I'd like to see your powers matched against. He is currently away at the Front, as is so often his want. When he returns, you will fight him."

Shango crossed his axes over his chest and nodded. "I will vanquish whoever you put before me, High General."

The next day, the clash between Thor and Shango created a sonic boom heard across the cosmos. The collision was not just of two ethereal bodies, but of two pure energy sources born of fire and lightning.

Ozone caked the air; electricity sizzled the stars.

Unwavering concentration etched into Shango's face, his muscles tensed with each of his blows. Thor had a flat forehead, his limbs loose, and his mouth hooked upward in a smile.

Shango hated that wry grin. And it only seemed to grow the longer they fought, more so when Shango felt he was close to victory. Twice he had spun his axes with the speed of shooting stars, casting off red lightning like viper strikes. Yet Thor evaded him—those attempts at attack earned howls of laughter from the warrior. Thrice Shango had closed the distance enough to land a pair of jabs and a single head butt. The latter even drew blood from Thor's lips, but the god simply wiped the crimson sheen away and whistled a light tune.

"Your bolts may dazzle the mortals, but your aim is as sharp as a drunken squirrel on ice!" Thor jeered with his Nordic accent. "Stick to shocking puddles, my friend, and leave the storming to the true God of Thunder."

Shango grunted and increased his efforts. Each of his fresh

attacks paired with great roars. It must've gone on like that for hours. They would fight, Thor would laugh, and Shango's anger redoubled like iron forged in fire.

The bout between them quickly escaped the confines of the camp—which by now they had left in utter shambles. Their audience moved with them from crater to crater, asteroid to asteroid, dancing among the gas clouds. It reminded Shango of the monkeys in the jungles of his old home. They too would swing from tree to tree to keep up with the action of a fight between their kin, just as the deities watching him and Thor now seemed to swing from the stars for the best view.

Zeus hooted the loudest after every sonic boom exploded in the air.

Shango's scowl deepened as Thor's boisterous laughter reverberated off the space rock. The mirth in the God of Thunder's eyes stung like a slap to Shango's pride, a silent insult that lingered in the air, unspoken but unmistakable. Zeus would put Shango in the vanguard along with Marduk if he didn't wipe that smile off the wretched Norse god's face.

"Let's see you laugh at this!" Shango grunted as he flung both his axes ahead of him in one powerful strike. Once more, Thor appeared to narrowly evade the assault and responded with a blast of blue lightning, accompanied by his distinctive guffaw.

"There's always something to laugh at." Thor spun around another attack and swung his hammer upward, carving an asteroid in two. "Like that beard of yours."

I have a beard?

Since testing his strength against the other gods and deities, Shango had forgotten to shave clean, as he usually did. He leaned his chin into his shoulder to feel the rough mustache and patch under his chin. The bastard was right.

Shango grunted, then captured the two pieces of asteroid Thor had bisected in a pair of lightning cages. But instead of flinging them out immediately, he let them swirl above his head. All eyes were on him. The longer the battle went, the more of a fool he was made out to be. He needed to do something substantial, something even this Mighty Thor could not hope to defend against.

"Hah! More! More!" Zeus bellowed from his floating throne. "Don't stop now, Orisha! You can do better than that!"

Shango was King of the Yoruba! He couldn't let himself be toyed with. It was utterly beneath him. Zeus might not have known his name before this bout, but Shango was as much a ruler as he, and he would make that known.

The Orisha pressed his lips in a thin line, his brow furrowed. After maintaining the asteroid fragments above his head, Shango set them free. They spun around Thor's head like a cyclone. His wife, Oya the Windweaver, would've been proud to see the exploit.

As expected, Thor bobbed and weaved with glee, and Shango allowed himself his first smile. As Thor did his dance, distracted by the attack, Shango stirred Ashe within his belly. It flowed through his arms and through his twin battleaxes. Instead of attacking Thor in a straight line, he lifted his weapons to the stars, and lightning rained down like a deluge.

No one was safe.

Zeus made off with his lovers behind the asteroids; the war deities took cover or protected themselves with their own glowing enchanted shields. Shango couldn't even see Thor between the large bolts that seemed to split the very heavens.

"Zeus, you fool!" a deity glittering with diamond skin called out from the side. "You've let this contest go on for too long. The Orisha will cause a fissure."

"Bah, this is the best fight we've seen in far too long!" Zeus replied with glee, though Shango couldn't tell from where. "Let them have their fun. And let us enjoy the spectacle!"

A great roar sounded from within the avalanche of lightning, followed by the greatest rumble of chuckling Shango had heard yet. He frowned. Somehow, Thor had matched his greatest power. Thor's hammer absorbed Shango's thunderstorm, causing the Thunder God's hands to shake on the weapon.

"The High General speaks true." Thor smirked through his words. "I've never met my equal in the storm. Orisha Shango, you may very well be my match."

Shango realized his error in that moment, his misjudgment of Thor's character. The Norse god was not some arrogant *òlòṣí*—well, not wholly, anyway. He was a lover of battle, just as Shango was. Shango had been too narrow minded in his goal to defeat Thor that he hadn't appreciated the thrill of their fight. If the rumors were true, no one had proven a challenge to Thor, just as no one in the Mortal Realm had proven a challenge to Shango. He couldn't remember the last time his Ashe coursed so fiercely through his body.

Had it ever?

With one last bellow, Thor unleashed the lightning he had absorbed in one single blast aimed at Shango's chest. But Shango knew lightning more intimately than his own breath, no different from Thor.

Evading the strike itself was a simple thing if it had been an ordinary bolt, but the supercharged combustion was as wide as a redwood, and it tore through the air and split across Shango's forearm, searing skin. Ultraviolet radiation blanketed the surrounding space. The bright light hung suspended in the air for several moments before it cleared away to reveal an actual tear through reality. And on the other side: a horde of shadows!

"God Eaters!" shouted a deity draped in an eerily tattered cloak.

Abandoning his lovers and uplifting his thunderbolt in hand, Zeus flew forward with murder carved on his face. "These are mere sentries. All of you, with me, before the Sovereign One senses the breach! Shango, Thor, come. You'll be my flanks. Let's see your strength levied on a true enemy."

The war deities broke up in formation with the military precision of countless ages. Squad lines manifested within the space of a few heartbeats.

Shango panted, sweat glistening on his shaved head. Slick perspiration made the cowry shells around his upper arm slip uncomfortably and he grunted, pushing them back into place. The scar carved in his arm throbbed. But he bit the pain away, took in a deep breath, and was ready to take on whatever these new enemy shadows were.

Thor tapped Shango on the shoulder with his hammer. "Zeus' flank on your first day, Orisha." He smacked his lips. "Not bad. When we win this battle, he'll make you a general. Mark my words."

"When?" Shango questioned, unsure of the foe they were about to face. "Not if?"

"Of course, brother! You give these God Eaters a mere piece of the fight you just gave me, and this will be over in minutes."

Shango wouldn't call Thor his brother in turn, not for several moons after that battle, stubborn as he was. But in that moment, he knew this cavalier Asgardian would become his closest comrade.

3

In the courtroom, Shango basked in the memory of the first time he'd met Thor. He lifted his gaze to find his wife, Oya, who smiled back at him nervously from the courtroom's public benches. She sat among the other deities that overwatched the trial, a collage of humanoids, creatures, and spirits. But Oya stood out stark among them all in her bright magenta wraps that lovingly snaked around her strong shoulders and arms. Shango had found himself in a precarious situation, but at least his woman was there with him. It was just unfortunate she had to see him in chains, unfortunate that she got dragged into this, to begin with.

As they gazed into each other's eyes, Shango's face softened with a tenderness that rarely crossed his visage as a warrior deity. Time froze in a quiet storm as they communicated a thousand unspoken promises of love and devotion through their locked gazes.

They had been split for eons, and Shango couldn't for the life of him understand how he could ever think it wise to leave her side for so long.

That reverie between his mate was broken, however, by the incessant chirping of Oshosi and the Justice Council. Now his fellow Orisha spoke within inches of each judge—personal space be damned—apparently making his points of Shango's defense more clear.

"I implore you to consider the intent behind his actions," Oshosi would say.

And one of the Council members would answer, "You speak with conviction, but we must also examine the consequences of his actions."

Shango would've represented himself were it allowed by the Court of All. He was the official arbiter of Divine Justice via his red lightning, after all. And for Shango, justice was not boastful, nor was it loud. For Oshosi, apparently, justice was a show of flamboyant hand gestures, melodramatic shouts, and exaggerated whispers. The Orisha spun on his heel so often and so harshly, Shango was surprised he hadn't carved a permanent valley into the marble floor.

"What are you doing, old friend?" Shango murmured to himself.

"You gotta give some of these Greek deities a show," Oshosi had told Shango back in his holding cell with the more serious tone he was used to. "I thought that was your style, Mr. Life-of-the-Festival. Trust me on this one. We can't allow these òlòṣí to throw one of our most powerful Orishas in their dungeon."

Because we need every warrior we've got, Shango thought.

Perhaps Oshosi had a point. The Orishas had been weakening over the past few centuries, just as Marduk had all that time ago... before the God Eaters overcame him. It didn't help that humanity had become so secular, had turned to technology as their new guide. But it was an expected outcome, a lose-lose situation the Fates had told them would be an unfortunate byproduct of their separation.

"When we asked for help, who answered the call?" Oshosi spread his arms wide as he spoke, his wood-like jaw working seamlessly over his practiced words. Shango snuck a peek at the audience behind him, to the other deities serving as witnesses. Most of them seemed as though they were suppressing groans. "*Shango* answered the call. Because that is what warriors do. Their greatest duty. Only death on the battlefield can bring them eternal purpose."

Oshosi cleared his throat for effect. He used silence like a hunter's trap. A moment of safety until he pulled the bait and savored his trophy. Only now the prize of his hunt was a majority vote, not bushmeat.

Twiddling with the bow at his back, Oshosi went on. "Great Council, if you'll allow me, I'd like to paint a picture. Imagine the cosmos of a distant realm blazing with fire—though this clash does not manifest in conventional explosions. While these combustions are abundant in streams of furious reds and crackling purples, those hues are swallowed instantly by the void of darkness."

One judge, the blue-skinned Yamaraja, scratched curiously at a tall crown of rubies. The buffalo he sat on snorted in what sounded like an utterance of "huh?"

Oshosi threw his hands up in defense. "Stay with me. This... cosmic picture I want to fill our minds with... to a traveling stellar ship or an alien star-worm, the collage of colors devolving into nothing at all would've looked like shooting stars dying in the night..."

Shango groaned. Was this really the best defense his pantheon could muster? Filibustering?

"... But for the deities of the Earth Realm, for you and me, those rainbows of radiance are far from a pretty sight. For thousands of years, this image has played on repeat. A war that never seems to end. A war in an eternal deadlock. An impasse."

Shango cleared his throat loudly, and Oshosi stopped his talking for a moment. It wasn't until Shango waved him over that Oshosi stepped back to the defense table.

"Is this the best you could do, Hunter?" Shango hissed under his breath. "Filibustering? Really?"

"Well, I'm working with very little," Oshosi murmured back. "But... if you let me bring up the Fates, as previously discussed."

"No, absolutely not," Shango said a bit too loudly. "Keep

Anansi out of this unless we absolutely need to bring him up. We do not understand his messages. It would only confuse the courts."

"So be it," Oshosi said, turned on his heel, and continued his nonsense.

Shango gave a sidelong glance to the prosecuting table: Thor's sons, Magni and Modi of Asgard. They both stroked at their braided beards and tapped their fingers with a rhythm that told of the grunts they were suppressing. Shango didn't have much of a personal relationship with them. They and their father had a tenuous relationship that revolved around Mjölnir—their father's signature weapon.

Thor had told Shango how he had been trapped under some jötunn or giant—Shango could never remember—and his sons were the only ones able to free him. One would think this would mean they were bonded for life, but when it came to an inheritance... many families across the realms, mortal and ethereal both, knew the precarious bridge that was the entitlement of heirlooms.

And when it came to that damn hammer, there was much love lost between father and sons.

One wouldn't have guessed Magni and Modi had any bad blood with their father now, what with how they scowled and snorted at each of Oshosi's words.

Damn if they aren't spitting images of their father though, Shango thought, a pang of grief stabbing at his heart.

"Speak plainly, Orisha," Modi spat through his reddish-blond beard.

Magni, with short locks of blond, nodded in agreement. "Do not speak in your flowery tongue."

They sound just like him, too.

"Order!" Themis commanded gently. "You will have time to speak shortly, Magni. Modi."

Oshosi did not waver. Clearly, he had practiced his speech and didn't want to change his flow. Was this the big play he wanted for the Greek pantheon in the audience? Was it even working? Shango took a peek behind him to find the himation-wearing gods were indeed leaning forward in interest.

"But the stars whisper, 'everything will be as it should be,'" Oshosi went on, "'for Shango and Thor are among us.' Now, I know many of the war deities present with us today would've said this battle we've found ourselves in should've been lost decades ago... Centuries ago, we lost Zeus to the Shadow Realm." He grabbed at his heart and took a knee. The Greeks seemed to appreciate that, nodding slowly in their grief. "Nearly two decades ago, after the Mayan deities' protective enchantments finally wore away," Oshosi gestured behind where a handful of the Mayans sat, "all thought our efforts would've been lost. You cannot deny that." Again, another silence for effect. "But Shango stepped forward where the enchantment had failed; Thor stood steadfast where others could not."

The Mayan deities shifted uncomfortably atop their benches, their feathered headdresses rustling.

"Shango would've rather been dancing among a drum circle," Oshosi put a hand to Shango's shoulder, and Shango stiffened as though a wasp had landed on his skin, "but when there was fighting to be had, he adapted his stomping feet for swift kicks, his rhythmic turns for twin-bladed flourishes. No one is as fast or as smooth as Shango, whose fighting prowess you yourselves have often likened to the strength of a lion and the speed of a viper." Oshosi mimed fighting gestures, sliding from side to side atop the floor like a fencer. When he finally stopped, he took slow steps to the prosecuting table, his next words for the Asgardian representatives. Magni and Modi only offered him twin frowns.

"Thor would have rather been drinking himself stupid over a never-ending kettle," Oshosi said, "but when the call to action came, he threw down his drinking horn for fists of fire, his drunken missteps traded for powerful overhand slams. No one was as strong or as resilient as Thor, a god who didn't know the meaning of the word 'quit'."

If Oshosi was trying to win the hearts of Thor's sons the same way he won the interest of the Greeks with his complimentary words, it was not working. Magni and Modi crossed their corded arms over their bulging chests with paired huffs.

Themis cleared her throat and rubbed at the edge of her blindfold. "I certainly hope there is a point to all this rambling, Orisha Oshosi."

"There is, High Judge Themis." Oshosi straightened. "I'm trying to establish Shango's good character, to establish his and," Oshosi inhaled solemnly, dramatically, "Mighty Thor's value to the warfront. How holding Shango as you are now is of no benefit to the repulsion of the God Eaters."

"We do not need your sweet words to judge character," Ma'at chimed in at the High Judge's side, her wings fluttering a touch. "We've Anubis for that."

"I'm very glad you've brought that up, Ma'at, seeing as that segues perfectly to my next point." Oshosi practically sang his words. "Something that'll ensure Shango is true of heart. I call my first expert to the stand: Anubis of the Ancient Egyptian Faith."

To anyone who knew Shango on the warfront, there was little doubt that his heart was noble and true. After the tear in the reality caused by him and Thor was stitched up—a feat requiring no less than seven sealing specialists and a full day's labor, Zeus made him general. Shango upheld his charge more truly than anyone could've expected. He did his duty, sacrificing the well-being of the mortals he used to overwatch. The mortals he was forced to leave on their own to be enslaved because he was fighting a battle with shadows.

How much had he sacrificed for his *own* personal love? Most of all, his favorite wife, Oya, whom he thought of every passing cycle amongst the stars. But he knew he needed to stop that. Thinking of Oya and all the others he left behind only shifted his focus from what really mattered. The Great War. If they allowed the God Eaters to get through, there was no future for any of them.

Only Thor knew this internal conflict of Shango. He and Zeus. The Greek Patriarch had tried to help in his own way too—with a host of sirens and nymphs, all of which Shango turned away. Instead, he kept his head down and fought. That was the only way forward. To turn off his heart and fight.

Shango's character was proven time and time again as he fought shoulder-to-shoulder with Thor for centuries in battle. Torment and guilt tore through him with every century that passed. And it was he and Thor who took up the mantles of General and High General respectively when Zeus was lost to the Shadow Realm in those early years for Shango, when the Fates split off from the rest of them, when the Mayans saved them all with their powerful defenses.

Shango would never willingly abandon Thor. Thor was the best man—best deity, rather—he knew. He was the type of being who would give you a free jab to his chin before starting a sparring match to "make things even."

That was a true brother.

4

In the past, on the day everything changed, Shango found himself scratching at the little beard he had grown. When he was mortal, when he was an Orisha made new, he had hardly cared for hair on his face. Beards were too itchy and too much food got caught in them. And though he had never confessed it out loud, he sported his first beard because of his kinship with Thor—a man whose beard was unmatched in both the Mortal and Ethereal Realms.

It was a typical quip about his beard that had started all the mess that would land Shango in the Court of All. Shango and Thor had been holding down the line near the Andromeda Front.

It was twilight then, the landscape of the asteroid fields glinting with the changing of colors. Where the crystalline rocks shone with the vibrant purples and blues of gas clouds, they became muted and desaturated as "night" fell. There was no time within the End Realm—not in the traditional sense. But the architects that constructed the space set up a day-night cycle for reasons unknown. Whatever the reason, Shango appreciated it. It reminded him of home.

And, like any other day, the shadows of the God Eaters were relentless, but Shango and Thor had made their battles with them a routine among the asteroid fields. Where Thor was too slow to uplift his hammer in attack, Shango was right there with his axes to make up the difference. Where Shango peppered their enemies with quick jabs of bolts, Thor would finish them with haymakers of lightning.

"Generals!" Raijin, the Japanese deity, called as he rode a gas cloud to their flank. His red and muscled skin glistened with sweat, and his usually disheveled hair was even more wild than usual. At his heels was his trusty wolf companion, Raijū, whose sharp fangs were matched only by his master's sword. "Generals! We have another fissure forming near the Crescent Moon Rock face!"

Shango twirled his axes in hand, already feeling the power within them stirring. "How much time do we have until it opens?"

"The revenant scouts say a half hour. Should I put a party together to handle it?"

"Depends." Thor stepped forward, his boots crunching space rock underfoot. "How big do the scouts think this fissure will be?"

"Minor. Only a Class-Five."

Class-Five was the most minor of threats. Nothing too concerning unless a shadow swarm was hiding behind the tear. Class-Three was a moderate threat. And Class-One was reserved for the sighting of the Sovereign One. That hadn't been called since Zeus beat the Great Shadow back into its Realm. And Zeus was never to be seen again.

Shango and Thor exchanged quick glances with each other. The battle at present was almost won. The Bolt Battalion had already wrangled most of the God Eaters in lightning cages across the asteroid fields for final annihilation. It was a better method than potentially letting the pesky sentries escape to wreak more havoc. But leaving now would mean setting all their efforts back a whole day. But a new fissure opening meant a whole new set of potential problems. It was like plugging holes in a sinking ship.

And any new fissure could theoretically mean the appearance of the Sovereign One.

"Raijin," Thor commanded, "you and your companion will take over for me and Shango here. You can call in my sons, Magni and Modi, as well. They'll be more than happy to take the glory if I'm not here to share in it. Shango and I shall take a war-band of Honorable Dead and make quick work of that fissure, then head back as you clean up."

Raijin bowed, his taiko drumsticks pressed into his hip. "Of course, High General!"

Shango knelt down to Raijū and gave him a pet behind the ear. His whole body was wrapped in lightning, but Shango knew the best place to shock it to give it the most pleasure. "Give 'em *Jigoku*, pup."

Raijū barked and wagged his crackling tail with joy.

"Come, Raijū!" his master said as he flung his taiko drums trap over his head. Raijū barked again. He and Raijin made their way to the others in the Bolt Battalion, leaving a trail of wind and lightning in their wake.

"You know," Shango said, "we really should think of getting animal companions of our own."

"I hear King Impulu doesn't have a rider these days," Thor replied.

Shango groaned. "Forget it. I changed my mind. I'd rather keep my head on my shoulders."

Thor laughed his usual laugh and *thwacked* Shango across the shoulder. "Come now, before the fissure gets big enough to let the Sovereign One in."

Shango and Thor approached the Crescent Moon Rock face just as the fissure took shape through a violet gas cloud. The scouts had said it would be minor, but to Shango's eyes, it was practically miniscule.

"That's it!?" Thor scoffed.

"Yes, High General," one of the revenants answered. He, like all the others, appeared as something between a corpse and a spirit —somehow translucent and corporeal at the same time, with an odd yellow glow tying his two forms together. The Norse had called them the Honorable Dead, former mortals that found themselves in Valhalla. This one looked like he had once been a Zulu warrior with his tall animal-hide shield and spear.

"I swear," Thor continued to laugh, "you scouts these days are getting a bit too antsy. This'll be child's play."

The revenant dipped his head in shame. "Of course, High General."

The Honorable Dead hardly ever showed their fear on their faces. Shango learned that early on. Their fear was often visible in the way they twitched their fingers over bows and jittered their grips around hilts. And just then, many of them had faces of stone with the body language of cornered dogs.

Shango couldn't blame them as he turned to the tear forming in reality, where God Eater shadows were doing their best to force their way through. Their shrieks were so fierce they echoed even in Shango's mind. For every battle, at least an eighth of the revenant ranks were lost. It took at least a score of mundane soldiers to vanquish one Eater, perhaps a little under a dozen if the revenants had an undead diviner or mage in their ranks.

For the Honorable Dead, their battles were fought by extremely slim margins. No room for error, unlike Shango and Thor, who could take a few shadow strikes and keep moving on. Sure, the hits stung like nothing else, but at least they could keep fighting. But if a revenant got hit, even by the smallest of cuts or strikes... that was it. They were done.

Clawing and snarling, the God Eaters strained against the fragile edges of the reality fissure, warping the air. Whispers and an unsettling aura escaped as the tear threatened to unravel.

Shango tuned them out as he addressed his band of soldiers. "Revenants of the Bolt Battalion. Hear me now. Steady your spirits." One of the God Eaters got one of its slithery wisps through the tear. "We stand on the precipice of the Great Void! But fear not, for we are the chosen guardians, guided by divine purpose. With courage in our hearts, we shall unite as one, wielding the power that banishes all Eaters. Victory shall be ours, for we fight in the name of the heavens! Onward, my warriors, and let our valor carry us forth."

A collective war cry sounded throughout the ranks. Its sounds rippled through the glow that surrounded each of the Honorable Dead. A rainbow of colors specific to each culture they originally came from. Those once quivering hands and fidgeting fingers were replaced by the steadiness of true warriors.

"Decent speech." Thor turned to Shango with a mischievous expression before going on. "What do you say about making this a little more... interesting?"

"Hmmm, what are the conditions and what is the bet?" There was always a wager with Thor. "I think I'm winning in the standings, aren't I? What's the count? My 3,072 wins to your 3,012?"

"That's because you cheat with those blazing-fast axes of yours," Thor said as a few more shadow wisps pressed through the tear. The Eaters would breach in mere moments. "Thus, you must give me the chance to catch up, my friend! Or are you scared I'll beat you this time?"

A palpable tension ran through the ranks of the revenants. Some of them edged their ghostly feet toward rock pillars and open crags for cover. This kind of talk meant destruction would soon follow, and they would be caught in the middle. They had died once. Most of them did not want to do it again. What waited was a death more permanent than their first. Sure, they might have been more powerful than ordinary mortals while in the End Realm, but the magic of deities dwarfed their abilities several times over.

"I never said anything about being afraid." A slight darkness entered Shango's tone. "Name the terms."

"Hmm..." Thor rubbed at his chin in thought, before snapping his fingers in excitement. "Let's role play for this one! I'll be you, and you be me."

Shango threw up an eyebrow.

Thor pointed to Shango's weapons. "For this next fight, I get to use those axes. And in exchange, you'll use Mjölnir."

"Hah! The victory is as good as mine, then." Shango had little confidence Thor could handle his twin axes. Without hesitation, he withdrew his weapons and offered them to Thor; Thor did the same with his hammer.

When Shango took the unfamiliar weapon in his hand, the weight nearly took him down to one knee. He bit back the grunt that threatened to escape his lips. He didn't need Thor telling him he needed to do more push-ups. Shango knew the stories of Mjölnir and the tale behind how Thor had acquired it. He had also heard rumor of the divine weapon only heeding those true of heart. This might've been Thor's play all along: to win the bet off the fact that Shango couldn't lift the hammer at all. In fact, that's *exactly* what Shango expected as Thor eyed him in a challenge that said, "go on, heft her up, then." The Norse god was already twirling Shango's axes in hand like a court jester.

Shango would show him. After all, they had an audience of gawking revenants.

Suppressing another grunt and flexing his veiny bicep, Shango made the slow move of lifting the hammer over his head. He did his best to make the concentrated effort appear as though he was toying with Thor. But in reality, the hammer felt like she weighed as much as a mountain. With one last heave, Shango stretched his arm out and let out one great exhale.

The revenants cheered and clapped, a rainbow of mist wafting from their bodies as they did so. A few slammed Trojan swords against their shields, others hoisted Medjay spears into the air, and some of the more modern revenants pulled rifle triggers aimed into the starfields.

Thor threw Shango's axes in the air, applauded his comrade,

and caught them again. "Good! You can wield her. I always knew you could. Now, there's one more condition to this wager."

Ugh, what now? Shango thought, but he kept his face neutral.

"We've got to do this with style," Thor went on. "We can't just use each other's weapons. We have to fight like each other, too. The Honorable Dead will be our judge. Isn't that right, lads and lasses?"

The revenants nodded their heads, humoring the Norse god.

"Hah!" Shango roared, loud and hard. "You couldn't match my rhythm if you tried."

"Then it should be another easy win for you, brother." Thor casually checked the nonexistent dirt under his nails. "The bet starts now." He brought his hand back and threw an axe just past Shango's head. It whistled by Shango's ear and straight into the amorphous figure of a shadow. Thor snapped his fingers and lightning blossomed from the axe, blasting the shadow into a shower of dark mist. Then the axe snapped back to his hand on the line of a bolt.

"Ah! So you *can* hurl these things like Mjölnir. I always wondered why you hardly threw them."

"Bah! That one doesn't count! That's not my style."

"Fine, fine. The contest is still zero to zero. I'll keep the axes in my hands."

5

AND SO THE BATTLE BEGAN. THE GOD EATERS THEY encountered were nothing but sentries—miniature versions of much nastier foes. One couldn't really describe their shape, as they were always changing as black and indigo shadows. They were always moving in a strange, almost ephemeral way. The only thing consistent about the entities were their terribly eerie cries that sounded like the wails of those they had previously consumed.

The sentries were more than just physical threats. Many of them sought to poison the mind with horrors before consuming the essence of their victims. They were more slippery than grandiose, attacking at different angles where they could.

"Steady yourselves, warriors," Shango grunted as he awkwardly lifted Mjölnir to strike against a trio of shadows that poured out of the tear. "Nothing we haven't seen before. You know, I think they might even be getting smaller. What do you think, Thor?"

"Definitely smaller. The screeching hasn't quieted down one bit though. Shall we shut them up, revenants?"

Lightning crackled around the generals and the revenants cried out in assent.

The protocol for Class-Five enemies like these was to take out as many as possible until they thinned out. Then and only then could one reseal the reality fracture with an enchantment every war deity had to commit to memory. Or else the bastards would keep coming, and the Battalion would have to mop up again. Shango was thankful for the easy pickings. Using Thor's hammer was more difficult than he thought it would be.

He did his best to imitate his friend's technique from countless hours of fighting by his side. First, by stretching out the hammer in his hand to promote flight. But that only resulted in an awkward flailing through the air charged with lightning. Shango soared haphazardly, which seemed to throw off the shadows that pursued him. They couldn't predict Shango's movements and neither could Shango himself. At least it culminated in more vanquished Eaters—style points be damned.

"Don't leave Mjölnir stuck in your hand, brother," Thor called out as he surfed an asteroid field infested with God Eaters. "She likes to be free. Give her a throw. She'll come back!"

As a rule, Shango made it a last resort to free his hands of his weapon, but he had seen how Thor boomeranged Mjölnir time after time. Plus, he knew he wouldn't hear the end of it if he didn't try.

"You can do it, General Shango!" one of the Dahomey revenants encouraged as she and her comrades worked together to trap an Eater with a mystical net. The cowries embedded in their crimson armor hides clinked with each of their movements.

Shango scowled as he blasted the net with lightning, helping the Dahomey to vanquish their pesky catch. He didn't need the optimism from the grunts though. It only made the situation more embarrassing. It seemed as though Thor was beating him in a count for kills, and there was a reason for that. Against such weak foes, Shango's much faster axes were better suited to the task.

Perhaps giving the hammer a stronger throw could remedy that gap in speed.

With an amateurish throw, Shango charged Mjölnir with

lightning and let her fly. He was shocked to find that an invisible tether connected him to the weapon. It wasn't like the way Ashe coursed through him and his axes but it was something similar, something just as deep. Instinctive. As the hammer pelted through gas cloud after gas cloud, she sizzled through every shadow she made contact with, forcing each to let out a terrible spectral cry. Then she did it again on the return trip.

Oh, Shango thought with a smirk, *I could get used to this.*

"Looks like I'm going to win this one, friend!" Thor shouted as he cut through two more God Eaters with lightning strikes. It was true, the shadows were already thinning out. "You had me chug a crater of beet juice when you won the last wager. It took me forever to get the red out of my mouth. This time, *when* I win, you'll have to shave that thing you call a beard. I don't need you embarrassing me the way you are with my hammer."

"Ah, but you've made a grave error, brother," Shango answered. "You've left too many of the Eaters alive. I'm going to catch up to you!"

But as the battle came to a close, the hammer in Shango's hand grew in weight. He nearly missed a few strikes, his arms slow to lift.

"What's wrong, girl?" Shango asked gently. "I thought you liked me?"

His words of concern didn't seem to help. Something was wrong. Something was tugging at him. But it wasn't Mjölnir as he first thought. This tug came from his body. No, his very soul. His Ashe.

What's happening?

"Watch out, Shango!" Thor shouted. "That one nearly got you."

Shango went on the defense, simply dodging the shadows that seemed to smell blood in the water. The fun and games were over. It was time to seal that fissure. Using the surrounding asteroid field for cover, Shango extended his free hand to begin the spell work to close the tear in reality. A few revenants came to his side to assist in the stitching. They weren't the best mystical seamstresses, but they could do a decent job until the experts arrived.

"Sealing the fissure already?" Thor laughed. "Ah, but we were having so much fun!"

The tugging within Shango grew stronger, pinched at the inside of his chest. Whatever was happening needed to stop. Now. The Eaters were coming within inches of Shango, slithering with erratic movements that changed their shape from mists to multi-armed creatures to horned beasts. Each jerk of transformation was more unsettling than the last. Like a beat of music that was just off-rhythm, peppered by the shadows' ghostly cries.

Shango had to envelop his body in a lightning cage to protect himself. But that wouldn't last with his power waning. Still stitching the tear along with the revenants, Shango flung out his lightning cage in a wider radius. It threw off the tiny Eaters who were no larger than Mjölnir herself.

But one got through, and time stood still.

Echoed whispers forced their way into Shango's ears. It was not the eerie cry of an Eater as he had expected, however. This sound was generated from something more familiar, yet more distant. A song he had not heard since the Fates parted ways from the other deities long ago. Then, in that stand-still moment, the stars jumped across the cosmos in a spider's web. Was it an omen of some kind? A warning against the obvious threat of the God Eaters... or something else?

In the split-second moment, the amorphous face of the God Eater changed briefly. Changed into the image of a face Shango hadn't seen in an age. The face of Anansi.

Was the Fate Deity among them?

As reality and the immediate danger of the Eater attack took shape once more, Shango gritted his teeth and strained as he lifted Thor's hammer. The tugging against his Ashe was too great though. The shadow was going to get him. A fear Shango was not often acquainted with forced its way through his body. He could count on one hand how many times he had been hit by an Eater.

There was a reason the number was so few. The pain that even one of those things could inflict on a deity was like a thousand pots of oil ripping through one's insides.

"Brother, move!" Thor shoved Shango out of the way and obliterated the last shadow, just as the tear stitched itself back together.

Thor's guffaw was so great that mystical lightning bolts flecked off his shoulders with each of his convulsions. "Oh, friend, you almost had me there. You're slowing in your old age. Too bad your boyish beard doesn't reflect that youth. Don't fret, though. I won't hold you to our wager. You've not much to shave away as it is."

Shango stared down at his hands, flexed his fingers. "No... no, something is wrong. Something stayed my hand on that last blow."

Thor sniffed the air. "You don't think one of those mind-rakers is around, do you? I thought we cleared them from the Andromeda Front long ago."

"Yes, High General, we did," the lead revenant, a female mage in glowing silvery robes, chimed in with unshakeable confidence.

Shango shook his head. "No, it wasn't in my mind this time. It was my essence. Like something was pulling my Ashe from within—"

Another image flashed before his eyes. Anansi's face painted in the stars again, only now his visage was younger. Wait, was that Anansi at all? The energy in Shango's belly pulled his attention to a star in the distance. No, not a star. Something bright and electric, yes, but fractured, stark against the dark of the cosmos. But no star. With its radiance came a sound, a voice that pestered Shango's ears like a grouping of flies to a lion.

"Brother." He lifted a finger. "Do you hear that?"

Thor pursed his lips and raised Shango's axes at the ready. "Odin damn them, it *is* those mind-rakers again."

"I don't hear anything either, High General," one of the revenants confirmed.

Another one added, "Neither do I."

"Could it be a message from the Fates?" asked a third.

Shango shook his head. They were wrong. He strained to listen.

I'm sorry I couldn't make it back, came a voice in his mind. A mortal boy's voice. *I'll find Shango... even... even if it kills me.*

What in Orunmila's Stars was that? Shango massaged his temples with vigor to force the voice out of his head.

"Brother." Thor raised his weapons in his hands, signaling for the Honorable Dead to make ready to attack one of their own. It wouldn't have been the first time. A severe sorrow carved its way through Thor's brow, and his tone darkened. "Brother, tell me what you hear?"

But Shango couldn't answer. He was in too much pain. In the distance, the bright light streaked like a bolt.

"Ugh," Thor uttered, "the bastards wield lightning now?" He took Mjölnir from Shango's hand and raised her overhead, generating lightning within her. He aimed the hammer's tip toward the odd light. "I'll get rid of it!"

"Wait! No! It's something familiar," Shango groaned. "Something... mortal." He pointed in its direction. He didn't believe his eyes, but it seemed as though the form of a boy was manifesting at the tip of the lightning streak. "It's not an Eater. It's a boy."

The stream of light grew in length—and in speed. It pelted straight for Shango's chest faster and faster until it was mere yards from him. It was clear the light was connected to a human boy. A mortal boy. One with pudgy cheeks and braids that whipped behind his head. Blotchy white streaks that must've once been dots covered his skin, making him look like a zebra from the Mortal Realm. Were those meant to be painted dots in observance of Obatala the Dreamweaver?

Shango took his axes back and raised them in defense. But the boy didn't zoom forward anymore. Instead, he disappeared. All was quiet. There was nothing left except the void of the Andromeda Front.

Then, suddenly, the boy bloomed from Shango's skin, straight out of his body as though he were giving birth through his chest cavity.

Shango roared; the boy screamed.

They continued their painful shouts until, finally, the boy plunged out and fell. The whiplash sent his braids over his cheeks and he tumbled to the asteroid below. He swept his hair from his face, revealing a pair of glasses over a wide nose. The eyes underneath the glass widened. Magnified.

"Orunmila's Stars..." the boy breathed out harshly, "i-it's really you! Y-you're Shango. The real Shango."

Shango lowered his weapons, rubbing at his chest in pain. "I-I am. A-and who might you be? How did you find yourself to be here?"

"My name's Ayodeji Oyelowo." The boy prostrated himself, his nose touching the craggy surface beneath him. "And long story short... your wife, Oya, sent us to find you."

A shockwave ran through Shango's body at the sound of the name.

Oya.

"Us?" Thor stomped to Shango's side with a questioning look, a few revenants trailing behind him, auras glowing.

"Holy s—" the boy named Ayodeji's eyes went wide again, exaggerated once more by his glasses. "Y-you're Thor! A-and," he pointed to Thor's hammer, "t-that's Mjölnir."

"Good to see you mortals haven't forgotten me and the ol' girl." Thor flashed a smile with a twirl of his weapon. "No wonder my power hasn't waned over the ages." Thor flung a thumb over his shoulders. "Most of these Honorable Dead don't keep their mortal memories, so I can never be sure. Tell me, mortal, do they still sing my—"

Shango threw up a hand. "Say that again, child. Did you say *Oya* sent you?"

"That's right. Said you could help us with a pretty huge problem we got with Olokun. He got out of his chains and is tryna drown the coast of Lagos, Nigeria."

"Lagos... what?" Shango titled his head in question.

"Oh, right. You don't know what 'Lagos' or 'Nigeria' are. Um... the western coast of the former Oyo Empire."

One revenant stomped forward, his full suit of a knight's armor clinking as he did. "Are we sure this isn't another one of the Eater's illusions, Generals? They've masqueraded as mortals and as the Fates before."

"'Eater's illusions?'" the boy questioned. "What's that?"

"It has to be an illusion." Shango reached out to touch Ayodeji's cheek. Odd. He certainly *felt* real. "I've only ever told of Oya to you and Zeus, brother. Zeus has been lost to the Eater's Realm for so long... They could be using information from him if they got into his mind." Shango spoke only a half-truth. Part of him wanted to believe this boy, to believe that he could feel the fire of Oya again. If he got back to her, could he really leave her a second time inevitably? He already hurt her once. Gravely. And there was no way to leave Ijọba Ipari without the Court of All breathing down his back. They'd have him in a cell quicker than a lightning bolt to the ground.

Thor considered Shango with knowing eyes. "Let's not be jumping to conclusions quite yet, everyone."

"Am I trippin'?" The boy rubbed at his eyes under his glasses. "What are y'all talkin' about? And what's with them rainbow ghosts standin' around you? Is that a bifrost thing?"

Thor took a knee and placed a hand on Shango's shoulder. "Your Oya is not something to be taken lightly. We should be sure about this, should we not, brother?"

Shango hadn't made it this far just to make it this far. He couldn't stray from his path, not when he had denied the Mortal Realm so often before. With each of those instances, he hadn't batted an eye. But in all of those cases, Oya had not been a factor. It made little sense that a mortal would be able to communicate with his estranged wife. The Great Separation was clear on that. No mortal—and no Orisha, for that matter—was able to connect with one another. It would be impossible for this Ayodeji to have any contact.

So, Shango asked, "Boy, tell me. How did you come to speak with Oya?"

"W-well... i-it's a long story, ya know." He gulped and spoke quickly. "First, Oya came at my friend Manny in New York, but Oya got trapped in Eshu's staff. Then the homie TJ helped us get up a golden chain to the Sky Realm to find her, but Eshu chased us away and—"

"Enough from you, illusion." Shango flicked his finger and flung the illusion away with a bolt of lightning the moment he heard "Eshu". The boy illusion went tumbling back and back and back until it receded into the cosmos from which it came. Nothing but fiction and deceit. Just as Shango had suspected.

"Odin's Spear!" Thor shaded his eyes, looking out to where Shango flung the boy named Ayodeji. "Is that how all you Orishas treat your worshippers?"

Perhaps Shango wasn't so true of heart...

6

Shango stirred in his seat nervously before the Court of All. His chains clinked together, wrapped under the Asgardian magic-suppressing ribbon called gleipnir.

He'd nearly forgotten how dismissive he initially was of Ayodeji Oyelowo not too long ago.

Between the public benches of the court rested a gilded fountain in the likenesses of the Justice Council. Each statue held their hands aloft, where water sprinkled from fingertips and fed into the basin below. Unlike a mundane fountain of clear blue water, this one, like the statues themselves, shined gold.

From the depths of the waters, Anubis rose without a ripple, revealing his jackal head and then his human torso. A set of scales rested over his palms. No drops cascaded off him, and he was surprisingly dry as he stood to his full height.

Shango had become far too familiar with the Egyptian god. He and the other Veil Walkers turned up anytime one of his comrades fell on the battlefield.

As Anubis stepped forward fully from the fountain, a pang of jealousy raced through Shango. The golden fountain was the only *authorized* way in and out of the End Realm. If only Shango was allowed to use the fountain to get back to the Mortal Realm to begin with, instead of using more secretive and unstable means. Perhaps then Thor would still be with them.

"Anubis," Ma'at called out from the high stand, her sun-kissed skin matching the golden-brown chair she sat upon, "please, approach with your scales."

Anubis did as directed, and Ma'at plucked the feather from her hair and handed it to her contemporary. The jackal-headed god peered over his shoulder to Shango. "I'll be needing your heart, Orisha."

Despite putting on his best mask, Shango's face faltered, slacking into a frown.

Oshosi lowered his voice in Shango's direction. "It'll only be temporary, friend."

Shango did not smile.

"You can have this jackal-head stick his hand in your chest," Oshosi said, "or we can bring up how Anansi interfered and—"

"Enough with that," Shango bit out. "I'm not afraid of this test. I am true of heart. Let's get on with it."

Oshosi shrug, his feathered headdress fluttering with the motion. "It's your funeral, old friend. Well... at least now you can know what it's like to have a near-death experience without the threat of actual death, eh?"

Shango narrowed his eyes at Oshosi to erase that silly smirk on his face. Shango knew death like a next of kin. Oya had once been the gatekeeper of cemeteries. He had no desire to willingly experience the sensation of death again, no matter how often he brushed against its veil.

"Come now," Oshosi gave him a slap on the shoulder, "it'll be over before you know it. And we need to get you out of this courthouse and back on the battlefield."

"Enough with the smiling and slapping," Shango gritted. "You need not perform for me like you did with the Greeks."

Oshosi cleared his throat. "Apologies, old friend. I'm getting a bit lost in this performance I'm putting on. Obatala told me about this method acting approach those mortal children taught him in the Sky Realm."

Begrudgingly, Shango stood. The bright, ultraviolet light slicing through the courtroom from the gas clouds outside forced a squint from his eyes. He made his awkward shuffle over to Anubis and Ma'at to offer himself to their justice—the action made more galling by the chains binding his ankles.

"What would you have me do?" Shango asked them.

"Since you are not dead, Orisha," Anubis explained in his husky voice, "you must lend me your heart... willingly."

"Very well." Shango stuck out his large, exposed chest, giving himself to the Egyptian god without protest.

Anubis waved his hands in the air, manifesting brown smoke that wafted with the scent of sandalwood. Eerie chanting filled the air. A duet hummed by Anubis and Ma'at. Shango tried to steel himself for the inevitable moment when his heart would be extracted. But despite his efforts to remain calm, he couldn't shake the unease that gripped him, wondering if his heart would be found wanting and he would be doomed to guilt.

It was an odd thing—the reflection that forced its way to the front of Shango's mind. He and the other Orishas didn't deal in morality like most of the other pantheons did. When he struck a jungle with lightning, it was not because he had a distaste for the trees. He was simply managing the balance between the negative and positive charges within Oya's clouds. And sometimes that balancing act materialized over an unsuspecting village. Did that make him a bad deity? Did that make his heart thrum false? Shango hadn't considered that much, but in that moment, it gave him pause and something like fear entered his spirit.

The rest of the ritual only took a handful of moments, with Shango standing firm, Anubis and Ma'at singing their hymns, and Oshosi fidgeting with the quiver slung over his back. The watching audience stretched long necks for a better look or rubbed overly large eyes to make sure nothing was missed. None were more keen for the results than Oya, who nearly slipped off the edge of the bench she barely sat on in the first place.

The sung hymns reverberated off the grandiose walls of gold and Shango felt somewhat more at ease, as though a soothing spell fell over him like a gentle sheet of silk. And—somewhere at the edge of hearing—several voices entered his ears. Familiar prayers he thought lost to the End Realm. Songs from his people. His worshippers. His heart hitched. Perhaps he wasn't alone in his judgment. Perhaps the sponsorship of his followers was factored in as well...

Before Shango knew it, Anubis' hand plunged deep into his chest, and in the next moment, Shango's beating heart sat in the god's palm. The action felt like being plunged into frigid water, as though his heart was some massive source of heat, and without it, he was left bare to the sensation of stark, glacial cold.

Oshosi had said the sensation would be like a near-death experience, but he was wrong.

To Shango, he *was* dead.

7

All sound dimmed in his ears. His knees buckled. His head spun. Just when he felt himself about to black out, Anubis sunk his hand back into Shango's chest, and Shango was whole again.

What had happened? Was he already judged? How much time had passed?

Shango's fluttering gaze skated over the scales that sat atop the high table. A bit of blood dotted one scale; the other, Ma'at's feather. Most importantly, the scales favored where the feather sat. From the little Shango knew of Anubis and his scales, Ma'at's feather weighing more than Shango's heart was a good thing.

Anubis bowed before the judges. "Shango's soul is uncompromised, free of any God Eater corruption. His spirit is true, though he may be riddled with guilt." He dipped his jackal head again, took his scales, walked back to the central fountain, and sunk into its golden waters once more. The god was always about his business. No fuss or fluff with him. Once his hearts or souls were reaped, he moved on to the next.

Shango too took his seat again, head still reeling from the alarming experience.

The red-headed Modi stood at the prosecutor's table, his

braided beard as stiff as his voice. "Good people and pious deities make poor choices, Great Judges." His height was almost enough to cover the large window behind him, which reflected a cluster of purple and pink space dust.

"The only valid judgment here is whether or not Shango compromised Thor's position against the God Eaters," his blond brother, Magni, added, "and whether he'll break his oath again, given the chance."

"This is the first I've heard you speak of your father in ages, young ones," Shango challenged. "I'm forced to wonder where this quest for justice is being born from."

Both siblings flexed their chests and neck muscles. It was Modi who spoke up first. "We would've spoken to him sooner, had you not stolen his attention from us all this time."

"Stole his attention?" Shango nearly scoffed. "Countless ages in Utenheim and you believe me capable of demanding the totality of Thor's attention? Let's not pretend your presence here is because of some desire for justice. Tell me, what would you gain from seeing me in chains? The God Eaters aren't going to let up anytime soon. And you two can't possibly think you can take up where your father left off, bold and brash as you are. I'm the best hope for the Battalion and you know it. You hate it."

Lightning flared behind Magni's eyes. "Speak one more word against us, old man, and—"

"And what? You'll shock me with that pathetic excuse for lightning you possess? I wish to see you—"

"Enough!" Themis interjected. Her voice always possessed a quiet finality. "Oshosi, control your charge. Now."

Oshosi waved his hands apologetically. "No offense meant by any of that, Esteemed Judges."

"Oh, no, I meant it." Shango didn't break eye contact with the brooding siblings.

Oshosi pretended not to hear Shango. "Tensions are just a little high so soon after Thor's passing. This is why I previously requested the date of this meeting be pushed back for at least another moon."

High Judge Inanna flitted her wings, her horns casting a long shadow across the courtroom. "Let us confer on Anubis and the weighing of Shango's heart."

"Of course, Great Inanna." Oshosi dipped his green-and-white feathered headdress in grace.

The seven judges' gazes flitted upward, giving their eyes an off-putting blank stare of white. This meant they were conferring with each other telepathically. Shango never had a good sense for that kind of magic, but sometimes, he thought, if he strained his ears hard enough, he could make out whispers in the still air.

"What in Orunmila's Stars was that, you fool?" Oshosi hissed with sharp stillness, leaning in close to Shango. "You act like a mute for most of the trial and *that's* how you decide to string together more than two sentences? Do you know all I had to do just to have this trial?"

Now *that* was the quiet spittled rage Shango had known Oshosi for. He caught a glimpse of a giggling Oya just over Oshosi's quiver and bow. Shango couldn't help smiling back. Oshosi caught the exchange and scowled. "Don't encourage him, Windweaver. This is a very serious matter."

A touch of an angry storm crept into Oya's gaze. "Is that what you call all that theatre and flailing about you were doing earlier?"

Oshosi grunted. "Like I told your husband. It's the Greeks, they love—"

"A good show." Oya shook her head, keeping her voice low too. "Yes, yes, I heard what you said to him before in his cell."

Oshosi was unfortunately right, though. It was a poor choice for Shango to lash out, as he had done. He just couldn't stand the false piety Thor's sons were playing into. And part of him wanted to coerce their true reasoning for being so against Shango when they barely spoke to their father—or to Shango, for that matter, despite being part of the Bolts.

"My husband and I do not play with words," Oya continued

in a whisper. "And in times past, neither did you. Does this Justice Council not have some trial by combat?"

Oshosi sighed. "Unfortunately, no. Not anymore. There are too few war deities in Ijọba Ipari for something like that."

Oya crossed her arms and sucked her teeth long and loud. "This Oshosi," she pointed at his bare chest, "I do not know him. You're acting more like Eshu."

Shango chuckled lightly. "That's what I was thinking earlier, too. You've even got his pudge." He poked at Oshosi's stomach. "How can you hunt in such a shape?"

Oshosi slapped Shango away with a deftness that told of his hidden strength. "The mortals barely hunt these days. They'll hardly pray to me when they have their factory farming now. Times change. We Orishas have been split and fractured. We have to adapt to remain relevant."

"Even more reason why this Court shouldn't be holding me in chains," Shango added.

"We're in agreement there, old friend." Oshosi turned his attention back up to the conferring judges, keeping his voice low.

After a moment more of the judge's ethereal whispers and telepathic considerations, Themis spoke. "The Council agrees, Magni and Modi of Asgard. Oshosi of the Yoruba, we need evidence of Shango's innocence, not evidence of his character. The question is simple: did he or did he not leave Thor and his unit compromised on the Andromeda Front against the God Eaters?"

"With all due respect, Great Themis," Oshosi kept his head low, his own peacock-looking headdress nearly sweeping along the floor, "Shango's character is what's being called into question today, is it not? We need to establish that to make it clear he'd never leave a comrade—no, a brother—to fend for himself against such a great enemy."

"You heard High Judge Themis," Yamaraja intoned deeply; his mounted buffalo huffed in agreement. "Her Word is final."

Oshosi fell silent a moment too long. It wouldn't have been so bad if it were anyone else. But considering how loquacious he had been before, the moment of pause was stark.

"You see, Esteemed Judges?" Magni flung a hand toward the defense. "They have come with no honest rebuttal. I think it's time we stop sparring with blunted swords here. Shango's spirit may be true, but his battlemind has been compromised at the very least. Or need I remind everyone who was responsible for losing Zeus to the Shadow Realm all those eons ago?"

Oshosi stepped forward. "Pardon me, I thought we were striking that from the record, Your Honors. Shango's name was already cleared of having anything to do with that tragic incident."

That had happened so long ago and was such a ridiculous claim. The notion of it being brought up had never even come to Shango's mind. Thor's sons were desperate. But why?

"Correct you are," High Judge Forseti of Asgard confirmed. "What happened to Zeus cannot enter this trial, sons of Thor."

Despite Forseti hailing from the same pantheon as Thor's children, he was incredibly impartial. Magni and Modi exchanged grave looks with one another. Forseti had remained quiet for much of the trial. For him to interject at this time was significant.

The pair nodded to one another subtly, but surely. "We have more," Modi confessed. "More to present to this Council."

"Go on..." Themis said leadingly.

With a wave of their hands, Thor's sons summoned the mighty Mjölnir to appear before the judges. The courtroom filled with a bright light as the hammer materialized in their hands. Her glow competed even with the sheen of the gold all around as she crackled with lightning and rumbled with thunder. Those on the public benches who were not as familiar with Thor gawked in amazement as Magni and Modi held up the hammer, presenting her to the Justice Council.

"And what does this mean, then?" Oshosi asked with an exaggerated pout. "We all know of the late Thor's weapon."

"Go ahead, General Shango," Modi grunted. "Tell the Esteemed Judges what you've done."

Shango genuinely had no clue what the red-headed fool was talking about, and he hoped his expression told the truth of it. "Tell them... what exactly?"

"How you set up our father's demise to take Mjölnir for yourself." Magni's expression darkened, but a wry smirk stretched across his lips. Shango's throat tightened. "Oh, what's wrong, Orisha? No more of that venom you showed the court a moment ago? Afraid the truth will out?"

"What is he talking about?" Oshosi murmured in Shango's ear.

"I truly have no idea," Shango muttered back.

"High Judges!" Modi clapped his hands, walked over to Thor's hammer, and lifted her with great effort. "I would like to present my father's weapon to each of you. Lift her. Move her around. Try your best to wield her as though she were a hammer of your own."

A few members of the council sighed and told the brothers to cut to the point. But a few others chimed in with a "now, hold on one moment" as they confessed their desire to prove their mettle against the hammer. Shango cracked a smirk at the more eager of the group. He imagined it was something many of them privately wanted a crack at, but most were too prideful to admit. Even the initial naysayers took part in the exercise... eventually.

The Justice Council gathered around Mjölnir, each with their own attempt at managing the famed weapon. Themis, Ma'at, and Inanna could barely even hold her for more than a moment before succumbing to her weight. Yamaraja, Issitoq, and Mithra had an easier time, but none of them could actually swing her like an actual tool of combat. Forseti, who was also of Asgard, was able to move her in a hammering motion, yet the gesture was so slow it seemed as though a sloth was wielding her.

Modi took Mjölnir back in his possession. "As you can see, the weapon is difficult to use. But that's to be expected. She's a temperamental tool. More than a weapon. More a divine instrument, really. A piece of my father himself."

He lifted Mjölnir above his head and swung it around in a circle, but, much like Forseti, all he could manage was a sluggish motion. He handed the hammer to his brother, Magni, who showcased the same slow movements. After they were satisfied with their demonstration, they set Mjölnir atop the desk of the defense, just before Oshosi and Shango.

"Go on, then, old man," Magni challenged. "Show the Court of All what you can do with my father's hammer."

8

So this is why Magni and Modi were so interested in Shango's imprisonment.

Shango could almost laugh if he wasn't taken so off guard. Even Oshosi was at a complete loss for words, and part of Shango wanted to give Thor's sons credit for that feat alone. Even Oya's flat-mouthed expression was that of shock. And the whole of the audience knew there was a shift in the vibrations between the golden pillars and arches of the courtroom. All that was left to fill the silence was the flow of water from the central fountain.

All these two irksome òlòṣí really wanted was Mjölnir's full support, something that obviously was lacking due to a certain Orisha.

Of course, Shango thought in shame, *of course it's that simple.*

Shango was never one to go for theatrics or exaggerated pauses. He already knew where this was leading, and there was nothing he could do to delay the inevitable. Mjölnir stared up at him, her runic symbols etched on her side, almost calling to him with their faint hues of lightning blue. Clearing his throat, Shango ran his chained wrists across the table, grabbed the grip of Thor's hammer, and lifted it over his head.

Mjölnir was as light as his axes, lighter than when he first lifted her. She felt like home, and the sorrow that had festered in Shango's heart seemed to melt away in light of the hammer's electric energy. It was almost as though he was linking hands with Thor himself.

A thunderous roar echoed throughout the courtroom, and the ground shook beneath Shango's feet.

In the hallowed chamber of celestial dignitaries, hushed tones rippled through the court as Shango brought Thor's enchanted hammer down. His movement held such grace that it left even the most skeptical among them momentarily silenced. Some of the Asgardians in attendance regarded Shango with arched brows that labeled him a cunning interloper; other gods exchanged knowing glances that spoke of rightful succession being claimed.

Modi snatched the hammer from Shango, but Mjölnir wouldn't give—like a child latched onto their parent's leg.

"That'll be enough, thank you," Modi gritted, face turning as red as his hair. Embarrassment entered his eyes as their audience's interest piqued at the struggle.

"Only if you ask nicely," Shango challenged.

Oshosi's voice came sharply into Shango's ear. "Òlòṣí, if you don't let go of that damn hammer..."

Shango didn't break his gaze with Modi as he told Mjölnir, "Go on, girl. Go back to the pups."

With a scowl, Modi hefted the hammer back into his possession, waved his hand, and disappeared Mjölnir into the ether. He sat back down at the marble table of the prosecution, clearly ashamed of the power play Shango displayed. Therefore, his blond brother, Magni, stood up in his stead.

Adjusting his armor plating and clearing his throat, Magni approached the center of the Justice Council podium. "For those who are not aware, Mjölnir is a family heirloom. After our father's passing, it was to be passed down to his eldest son." He pointed to himself. "Me. So you can understand how surprised my brother and I were when she did not heed me, as she should when we retrieved her. And it wasn't until some of the revenants approached us that we realized what betrayal had occurred. As you all have seen with your own eyes, Shango has swindled possession of our family right for his own gain."

"That's not how it happened," Shango interrupted bitterly.

"So you deny exchanging weapons with our father?" Modi came in to tag-team with his brother. "Revenants. Please, speak up and tell us what occurred."

The ghostly rainbow figures of the revenant scouts stood near the back of the public benches. "Yes, sirs. Magni, sir. Modi, sir," one of them, a Tomahawk warrior, said earnestly. "Shango used Thor's hammer and Thor used Shango's axes."

"It was a wager... a game," Shango tried to explain. "Esteemed Judges, I know how this looks, but I didn't know Mjölnir would only heed me after the exchange."

"It was a game you suggested, General," the Tomahawk warrior confessed.

Shango's heart dropped a little. He couldn't believe it. The Honorable Dead never lied. They couldn't. Not while in the confines of the Court of All. None of the lesser beings could speak falsehoods within its walls.

"What is this?" Shango questioned. "Tell it true, revenant. It was Thor who suggested we exchange, not me."

The revenant's face went completely still, unmoving, as he said, "It was you, sir."

Shango tore his eyes from him and threw his gaze at the high table. "Esteemed Judges, that is simply not true. The Honorable Dead can't speak false. This one has been compromised."

"With what power?" Magni asked, stroking his golden beard. "We don't have the ability to alter minds or break the enchantment the All-Father set upon the Honorable Dead." His hand moved from his beard to a crow's feather wrapped around his neck. His brother mirrored the movement, also wearing a crow's feather over his heart. Shango narrowed his eyes. Something here was off.

Oshosi chuckled darkly.

"What's so funny, Orisha?" Modi sneered.

A steady shadow fell over Oshosi's face. All mirth gone. "Funny may not be the correct term, son of Thor. The word I'm looking for is... juvenile." He did not continue or elaborate.

Magni quirked a blond eyebrow, looking at the judges and the audience to see if they were making sense of all of this. "And what exactly here is juvenile?"

"This," Oshosi stretched out a flat hand, palm up, "this 'evidence' you're presenting as some realm-shattering revelation. You've even given Shango here a stir. But all you're doing is proving our previous point. Anubis has deemed Shango's heart pure. Now Mjölnir is doing the same."

Themis considered Oshosi's words and turned to Thor's sons. "The Orisha is correct. This only strengthens Shango's claim. What are you getting at, sons of Thor?"

Again, the brothers traded dark looks. They knew what they were after; they just wanted to see Shango squirm.

"Your Honors," Modi said strongly. "We do not suggest this lightly, and we do not deny the deep character and power of the Orisha Shango. It is true he would be a great loss if he were not on the battlefield. But he is faltering. He dismissed one of his own mortals, thinking he was an illusion. He is responsible for the demise of more than one of our strongest deities, both confirmed and unconfirmed."

"Purity is a perception, an opinion," Magni added. "Mjölnir could be detecting the heroics Shango displayed on the Mortal Realm to help his worshippers. Same as Anubis. Noble as that act was, we all know where the true war lies. Here. In Utenheim. Shango may have a true heart of a warrior, but, Esteemed Judges, we need soldiers who can take orders and not venture out on their own volition. Those who do not betray their brethren, as Mjölnir proves. So..." He shared one last nod with his brother. "We wish to invoke the Channeling against Shango."

The grand courtroom fell quiet as the weight of Magni's words sunk in. Gasps and whispers skittered through the crowd.

Some of the more emotional and empathetic deities burst into tears. Shango steeled his face into one of anger.

Oya shot up from her bench and roared with the force of a thousand winds. "How *dare* you suggest such a thing! The Channeling is meant for traitors and thieves. There are *no* grounds for it here!"

Even Oshosi raised his voice before he reeled himself in. The Channeling had only been invoked a handful of times during the Great War. It was something each of them had agreed to when they enlisted. An unbreakable pact. They weren't just bound by the End Realm itself, but to one another spiritually. One couldn't just abandon the fight like some mundane soldier on the Mortal Realm. Even if Shango had intended to leave his post deliberately for some nefarious reason, he wouldn't have lasted long on his own.

But he *did* come back, and he was willing to fight for the others as he had done for eons already. To honor the memory of his fallen brother.

He shook his head. The judges couldn't allow this. The Channeling ensured that each deity's power could always be used for the war, even if they reneged on their pact. And, in the event of an ultimate transgression, they could invoke the Channeling, stripping the magic from the spiritual body, leaving nothing behind but mystical ashes. It would leave a deity's identity void, but their magical essence still divided among those who remained.

Shango swallowed thickly. If Magni and Modi truly believed he was in possession of Mjölnir, the best way to reclaim her was for Shango to be wiped from existence. Utterly.

"Mjölnir's sponsorship of Shango isn't a good enough defense on its own," Forseti said, leaning his head forward enough for his long beard to fall over his podium. "It could be that she is sensing Thor's fondness for Shango. But we can verify this notion." He snapped his fingers and Thor's hammer manifested before him. "Mjölnir, take a quick trip to speak with the dwarves. We need to make sure you've not been compromised in any way."

Mjölnir tipped her edge in a nod, drifted to the fountain, and dipped into the golden waters.

"Well," Oshosi whispered in Shango's ear as the commotion around them surged, "they won't bite on your good character. And this business with Thor's hammer will take more time than we have. Those dwarves always take their sweet time with their artifacts. I know you don't want to go this way, but if the Channeling is being cast about, we'll need to throw poor old Anansi and the Fates to the hyenas. After all, it's them or us at this point, old friend."

The Orisha had mentioned doing something like this when Shango had brought up his recent dreams and encounter with Anansi. Well, not a direct encounter. More like a message deciphered through the stars, like all the cryptic messages the Fates claimed they had to adhere to. But it was a piece of information Shango wanted to sit on. The once strong alliance between the war deities and the Fates had broken down quickly over the ages, and there was no need to foster further conflict.

Shango couldn't remember the last time he'd interacted with any of the Fates directly before crossing paths with Anansi. The Fates were a group of inaction as far as Shango was concerned, more willing to sit on their enlightened clouds and negotiate the stars for the right time to move instead of entering the fight and dying as many of his comrades had done. If other pantheons had followed the Fates into inaction ages ago, the Mayans would've never established their first proper defenses, Zeus and Thor would've never repelled the Sovereign One back to its Shadow Realm, and they'd all be dead by now.

Deities and mortals alike.

But at the same time, it seemed as though everything fell into place with the Fates, that everything that happened so far was meant to happen, and they only meddled when things steered off track. And Shango had to respect that.

He and Thor had spoken about the subject often, with Thor explaining that the Norns were the ones to first introduce the concept of Ragnarök to Odin. The Asgardians tried time and time again to prevent the event, seeking the Mead of Knowledge, throwing Jörmungandr into the sea, binding Fenrir, and all the rest. But in doing so, they unintentionally caused many of the scenarios of Ragnarök to play out just as predicted.

Oshosi cleared his throat and addressed the judges once more.

This was it. The defense Shango hadn't wanted to come to. Would they be subverting Fate as the Asgardians had tried and failed to do? Or were they playing right into their Divine Hands by bringing them up?

Oshosi pierced each judge with a critical eye. "We have more than just Shango's character to go on, Esteemed Judges. There is evidence of other foul play at work. Foul play this council is unfortunately deeply aware of. The Deities of Fate."

9

Both the judges and the audience stopped shouting at one another and leveled all their attention at Oshosi. Raucous voices transformed into murmurs skittering along the walls and throughout the grand hall. If Themis hadn't been wearing her blindfold, Shango would've bet his best cowries that her eyes were bulging.

"This is a serious topic and accusation." Themis settled her expression back to its usual neutrality.

"Well," Oshosi jerked his head to one side, "these are serious charges."

"We've not heard from most of the Fates for quite some time," Yamaraja added. "What makes you think they are responsible for the demise of Thor, and why would they use Shango as their fool?"

Oshosi took to his stage again, lifting an arm like a play actor before an eager crowd. "It is true that Shango abandoned his post, but not for selfish reasons, as he's being accused of. He was forced away because he thought a new fissure was being breached. So he pursued it. By the time he realized he was being led through a wild bushrat chase, he found himself near the Triangulum Front.

And at this place, he was met by none other than Anansi of the Akan himself."

It was a half-truth, a compromise they had come up with so that Shango could go free without compromising what the Fates had planned. It was a dangerous plan, but their only option.

Again, Oshosi laid the trap of another deliberate silence. This time he held it, not allowing it to be broken until someone else did it for him.

It was Ma'at who obliged, her deep and painted *kohl* folding curiously. "And... what did Anansi say to Shango?"

"He told him that Thor had to die for the guided Fate to take shape."

It was a guess, but a good one. They hoped.

"Liar!" Modi pounded a white-knuckled fist into his table that cracked it in two.

"That statement must be false," Magni roared in chorus with his brother.

"Esteemed Judges," Oshosi interjected, "if I was given the chance to continue, I would've been able to explain."

Forseti massaged his impossibly large beard with an inquisitive stroke. He continued to lean forward, his gilded crown falling into the light.

Oshosi was right again. Bring up the Fates and you got everyone on the edge of their seats.

"Go on, Orisha," Forseti said softly, peacefully, "tell us how Anansi conveyed this message."

Oshosi bowed. "Thank you. Anansi swindled Shango by weaving a tale through the stars. To our hero's eyes, he saw the potential of another God Eater breach."

"More lies!" Modi bellowed again. "The other members of the Bolt Battalion would've seen Shango venturing away from their position."

"We've a theory about that, Esteemed Judges." Oshosi didn't miss a beat, anticipating the retort from Modi. "This image Anansi weaved for Shango was for Shango and Shango alone.

And with the Battalion's attention occupied on the shadows, the unit did not give Shango another thought until it was too late. Until he returned. It's possible illusions were built for Thor and his unit as well."

"It does fit Anansi's typical modus operandi." Themis inclined her head. "His abilities afford him the gift of story and deceit, no?"

"You are very correct, High Judge," Oshosi said. "This is why we believe he—of all the Fates—was sent. Only he would be clever enough to pull Shango away from his closest comrade, and had enough kinship with the original Akan and Yoruba mortals to be closely intertwined with our pantheon."

"Aha!" one of the gods called out. "We knew the Fates could not be trusted!"

Shango shuddered. "This is why I didn't want to bring this up," he muttered to himself. "We have to put our faith in the Fates. We must..."

"Brother, are you saying that to give meaning to Thor's death?" Oshosi murmured back.

"Not because you believe in the Fates themselves," Oya added from behind.

Shango's only answer was a frown.

Modi and Magni finally unclenched their fists atop their table. They must've heard the tales of Anansi and his past exploits as well. It would seem, for the time, that they were buying Oshosi's story, perhaps even feeling guilty for accusing Shango of nefarious acts. Well, the latter was a slim chance. But even so... Everyone present seemed to take to it, in fact. Where before Shango had been pierced with sharp looks, now the faces in the audience were softening. The expressions written on the judge's faces were less apprehensive and more curious.

"Why not bring this up before?" Themis asked at the head of the high table.

"Frankly, High Judge, the Fates can be easily misunderstood," Oshosi answered. "The tensions are great. We wanted to build a bridge to the Fates, not continue burning one between them. We are sure they had their reasons, as they always do. We were hoping a test of Shango's character would be enough and we could figure out the rest on our own."

It was true. The tension between most of the deities and the Fates had been uncomfortably tight, near breaking. Everyone suspected their philosophical differences would eventually lead to active conflict between the two factions. And it seemed that day had almost come.

But was this fair to the Fates? This half-truth Oshosi fabricated could've been the breaking point. It had to be done to prevent messing with whatever the Fates had planned while still getting Shango off his charges. They were losing the war. Just as he had said, they needed allies, not more enemies.

Magni turned a low tone toward Shango, his pointed finger aimed at Oya. "Well, that still leaves Shango's wife. No one can deny that he brought her to Utenheim without authorization. Shango is not a judge and administrator. Bringing a new deity into the fold must be decided by our Divine Council, not a warrior. We should include her in the Channeling as well, to make up for those we lost alongside my father."

A thousand fires flared up in the pit of Shango's stomach. Heat sizzled throughout his whole body. They could accuse Shango all they wanted, they could even cast the Fates in doubt. But when it came to his wife... that was *completely* off the table. And he made a promise to stay true to her above all else. It was time to make good on that.

Fine, it'll be the full truth then, Shango thought.

"That's not... *exactly* how things transpired, Esteemed Judges." Shango sat up, the shackles around his wrists and ankles clinking. "I would like to take the stand... for my confession. My *full* confession."

10

Oshosi turned on Shango with eyes so violent they could've ripped through even the God Eaters' Sovereign One.

Amidst the grandeur of the celestial assembly, Shango stepped forward, his footsteps echoing through the hushed hall. All eyes, gleaming with an otherworldly intensity, fixed upon him as he ascended the opulent golden stand. His heart pounded, torn between the gravity of his confession and the impending consequences. The weight of every deity's gaze bore down on him, each glance a testament to the import of this moment.

A conflicted furrow marked Shango's brow as he grappled with the ramifications of his admission. Whispers of uncertainty and anticipation danced in the air, as the subtle currents of fate and destiny intertwined in the delicate balance of celestial power. He couldn't help but ponder the turbulence that his revelation might sow among the Fates and the War Gods, the delicate tapestry of divine relationships at risk of unraveling.

And yet, resolute determination shone in Shango's eyes, a fire that burned brighter than the trepidation that sought to quell it. In that pivotal moment, with the weight of gods and eternity upon his shoulders, he knew he could no longer evade the truth. As he drew in a steadying breath, all the realms seemed to hold their breath with him. The outcome of his confession poised on a knife's edge.

Shango did not stutter as he explained the appearance of Ayodeji Oyelowo.

"Yes, we are aware that a mortal appeared to you not long ago," High Judge Themis said. "Many of us here had personal conversations with the boy. What we fail to understand is what this mortal boy has to do with you, Thor, and the unsanctioned transport of your lover."

"I'm his wife, not his lover!" Oya spat from the public benches, but the thin line between Themis' lips shut her shouts down to a quiet scowl.

"The mortal boy is the reason my brother is no longer among us," Shango confessed.

Modi stood up from his table. "Are you trying to say a mere mortal took down my father?"

"Don't be ridiculous. No. No... Something far, far worse. Something your cohorts—your Norns—had prophesied long, long ago."

THE NIGHT AFTER ENCOUNTERING THE MORTAL BOY, Ayodeji, Shango had been cursed with some of his worst nightmares.

No, not nightmares.

Premonitions from the Fates.

In Shango's slumber, he stood among a vast, starlit void, watching as the stars spun a web across the sky. Something deep within told him this was no ordinary web—it was an omen, a warning of things to come. But what did it mean? Shango cared little for astrology and its riddles. His dream might've been some warning from the Great Beyond; he just couldn't begin to decipher it.

As he pondered the gibberish code, a presence stirred behind him. Turning, he found three figures standing in the darkness, outlined by the stars in the form of individuals Shango thought he might've known. They gazed at him solemnly, and one spoke, but the words came forth without a voice. Shango bellowed in frustration at the void, and his shouts went unanswered. The figures faded away as he raged all the louder until he found himself bolting upright, awake.

The dreamscape of stars transformed into the dark and tattered cloth of his tent just above his cot.

Why have the Fates come to me? he wondered.

He could not deny their presence now, first what happened at the reality tear by the Crescent Moon Rock, and now these damned dreams. The two were too similar, even if they made little sense.

Apparently, Shango hadn't been the only one to dream that night. He and Thor's sleeping tents were mere feet from one another. And as the grogginess of sleep left him, the shouts and grunts of Thor entered his ears.

Shango was up and out of bed in a flash. In a rare occurrence, one of the healers, Wong Tai Sin, beat Shango to the mouth of Thor's tent. Endless rows of canvas housing other warrior deities backdropped the Taoist deity. All of it rested atop a floating island among the stars.

Shango waved Wong Tai Sin away. "I'll handle it, Healer."

"Are you sure, General?" he questioned, his wide navy and indigo robes billowing mysteriously in the windless air. "High General Thor's screams have only grown worse. The others whisper fears of the Eaters meddling with his head. They heard what happened out near the tear today with that illusion of the mortal boy."

Shango was trying to forget about the illusion that had come to them that day. It only sent his mind back to Oya, back to the Mortal Realm.

"Healer," Shango started, "are you familiar with Jörmungandr?"

"The giant sea serpent of Norse origin, also known as the Midgard serpent, said to encircle the entirety of the Mortal Realm in times past?"

"And one of Thor's fiercest rivals," Shango clarified. "I can't tell you how many times he's encountered the creature and barely made it out to tell the tale afterward. With an enemy like that, it's not surprising for one to be plagued with nightmares. But his recent dreams have been more than that. They are visions, something that had long been prophesied by his people. It was the fate of death that had come for his uncle Loki and his half-brother Heimdall, who murdered each other in the early days of Ragnarök. It was the fate of death that will one day come to Thor, according to him...."

Shango frowned at that, cutting himself off as he realized something. Thor had said he had come to terms with his demise long ago. It was the reason he found joy in every battle he could take part in. It was perhaps why Shango, in turn, cherished every fight and wager and verbal jab he could with his brother, though he never mentioned it out loud.

Thor's grunting and shouting started up again, bringing Shango and Wong Tai Sin's attention to the mouth of his tent once more.

"Are you sure you will not need me, General? I can at least quell the torment."

Shango bowed graciously. "I am sure. I'll summon you when needed."

"Very well." Wong Tai Sin dipped his head, then retreated to another tent in need of his attention. Shango waited until the healer was out of sight before entering Thor's domain.

Thor's tent was a simple area, a round space with a round cot. Red banners depicting his fallen kin and comrades—Zeus chief among them—lined the edges. Thor had told Shango he always wanted to be reminded of those they had lost.

Shango rushed over to a basin filled with water and dipped a cloth in its depths. He brought it to Thor's forehead to keep his warm head cool. Thor's yellow hair stuck to his forehead like a paste. Shango eased his comrade's bangs away to better cool the skin.

If any of Shango's contemporaries witnessed this moment, they wouldn't believe it. He was known for his aggression and mighty will back on the Orisha Planes, not his newfound quality of caretaking. He'd only shown such a side to his wives, and even then those circumstances were few and far between.

If Oya could see him now.

Your wife sent us to find you, that mortal boy had said. No—that *illusion* had told him. *Said you could help us with a pretty huge problem we got with Olokun.*

Shango had nearly forgotten about the Mortal Realm and the Orisha Planes he had left behind. He had resolved that he'd never see Earth or his people ever again. It was the sacrifice all the war deities had made all those centuries ago—or was it a millennium at this point? Shango couldn't be sure. But hearing the names "Oya" and "Olokun" had given him a thing or two to ponder on.

Thor's violent coughs disturbed Shango's musings. He had finally come out of his nightmare, it seemed. When he opened his blue eyes with an embarrassed expression Shango had become too familiar with, Shango gave him a scowl. "Was it that wretched serpent again?"

Thor groaned in answer. "Aye. I was about to take my ninth step. Jörmungandr visits me at least a few times a night these days."

It had been foretold for such a long time that Shango had it etched in his mind: After taking a fatal and poisonous strike from the giant serpent, Thor was prophesied to only have nine steps before the poison took hold and ended his life. He and Shango had gone over so many scenarios that would allow him to live his days without taking those steps, including a wheelchair that Thor always scoffed at.

"You've nothing to fret," Shango said. "The beast can't get into the End Realm."

"That mortal of yours did."

Shango stayed quiet.

"Speaking of which, your child also appeared in my dreams and..." Thor stumbled to the anvil in the corner of his room. "I think I finally know why I made this." He held up a copper ring imbued with runic symbols. "I couldn't make sense of it before, but the inspiration to create this, this Lyn Ringe, was intermixed with the image of that boy. The Norns could be calling to you as well, brother."

Shango grunted, ignoring Thor's words. He didn't want to think about the illusion or how it had brought up Oya just to tempt him. So he redirected the conversation, saying, "Anything different about this new premonition with Jörmungandr?"

Thor nodded, dropping the ring in his pocket. "Only the location. It's taking greater shape. Our fight wasn't in an ocean but among floating rocks and gas clouds."

"Here!?" Shango questioned, alarm in his heart. "In the End Realm? When are you going to talk to Morpheus about these omens? I told you to go to him moons ago."

"There are no 'moons' here, brother," Thor grunted. "How can I tell the passage of time?"

"Do not play coy. You know my meaning."

Thor scoffed and took steps closer to Shango. "I'll not be toyed with by that pixie harlot. My mind is my fortress."

Shango sighed as Thor dropped to the floor and began doing push-ups—his way of "*burning off the nightmare sweats,*" he had said once.

"He's very good at what he does," Shango frowned, "and he would not take kindly to you calling him a 'pixie'. You can just talk to him. He doesn't have to tinker with your dreams themselves. Even Wong Tai Sin wants to help."

Thor didn't respond, instead grunting louder with each push-up.

"Fine, then." Shango discarded the rag in his hand and dropped to the floor with his palms flat. In the time it took Thor to get through one-hundred push-ups, Shango cleared two. This only served to motivate Thor further, not wanting to be outdone by his comrade. When Shango cleared 20,000 push-ups and Thor surpassed 18,000, the ground beneath them shook with lightning and quakes, eventually sparking flame to the tent. It was as though both were unleashing a rage they could not contain, a rage manifested in yet another competition. Thor was blocking out his dreams; Shango, his past life.

Together, they were unstoppable in their ire.

Neither of them noticed that the tent had burned away, and they had gathered an audience.

"Told you it was these two again," one of the deities mumbled from within the group. "This is just like the first time they met."

"At least this time there's no deluge of thunderbolts," chimed in another.

Exhausted and coughing, Shango and Thor fell on their sides. Before them, the other deities, small, wide, and large watched them with lifted brows—if they had brows at all. Shango's attention was locked on the center of the group where Wong Tai Sin held a boy by the scruff of his robes.

"I see you two have ruined yet another sacred tent." He scowled, then lifted the boy with irritation. "This one says he belongs to you, Orisha."

The familiar boy with braids on his head gave a meek wave and a slanted, bashful smile. "Maybe we got off on the wrong foot. I'm not no illusion from whatever the mind-rakers are, I swear. Can we start over?"

11

THE MORTAL BOY, AYODEJI, WAS BROUGHT AMONG THE MESS hall of the war deities. The space had been built for giants, with its pitched canvas raising several hundred feet in height. Round tables—some the size of Ferris wheels on their sides—littered the area. Each one played host to a combat unit and an assortment of offerings mystically transported from the Mortal Realm.

Shango had nearly forgotten how small mortal children could be. The boy sat in the middle of the room with a jaw that dropped to his knees, dwarfed by some deities that were ten times his size. But to Shango's surprise, the tiny boy was the center of attention.

"So you say mortals communicate with each other from long distances on something called... tele-cones?" asked a kneeling Lugh, who leaned on a spear that nearly brushed along the canvas roofing.

"Tele*phones*. And yeah, it's pretty dope!"

"And did I hear you right when you said the mortals fly on soaring boats? What happened to all the dragons?" asked the Japanese deity, Ryūjin, in their dragon form.

"That was a clouded invention," Ayo said. "Us diviners didn't make those. There's still a few dragons here and there, though, but they're in hiding. At least, that's what my friend from Osaka said when I visited Japan last autumn."

"Clouded?" Thor questioned, resting his chin on his hammer where his beard fell over it. "What's a... clouded?"

"Oh, that's what my people call the non-magical folks in the Mortal Realm."

All the war deities surrounding the boy let out a simultaneous "oooh." Then they started rattling off another series of questions, which the mortal child was more than happy to answer.

"Man, how long have y'all been up here?" Ayodeji slumped back in a chair twice his size—it was the smallest they could find. "I mean, the elders talk about the Great Separation, but.... they say that's 'cause Olodumare got mad at us diviners and went off to wherever. What y'all doing here, anyway?"

"Fighting the war of all wars," Shango spoke up for the first time, his voice grim.

"The Great War," Thor added. "My people called it Ragnarök. Though some of my comrades debate whether what we've been through is actually Ragnarök or not."

"Damn..." A sudden and deep sadness fell over Ayo's face. But it was unlikely he could fully comprehend the full crushing weight of what the Great War actually meant. "But you guys got all the muscle out here. There's a grip of war gods just in this mess hall."

"The God Eaters devoured almost all of our destroyer gods already." Shango pulled an offering plate closer with a single finger. The plate housed an assortment of red foods: red apples, red palm oil, red chicken, red crab, with a side of yams, corn, and red peppers, of course. "Shiva of the Hindu was the first to be devoured. Then Ammit of Egypt. Khaos of the Greeks."

Thor grunted. "Hm, Ammit. I almost forgot about her. She used to say she and the Eaters were alike, in a way. Where she was the devourer of the dead, they are the devourers of magic. The Eaters see us as the dead that simply need to be devoured. Simple-minded. Singular in their aims."

"Oh, shit..." Another sadness forced Ayodeji's mouth into a strong frown before he went on. "Is that like Owuo? At Ifa Academy, we learn a lot about the Akan deities. Like Anansi and Owuo. Owuo is the destroyer of mortals. So you're saying these... um... God Eaters are destroyers of magic?"

Shango nodded. "Destroyers of ethereal existence. They must be stopped above all else."

Ayodeji frowned, leaving a space of silence before he bit his lip. "Not to sound rude or anything. Everything here seems very important, but I don't have a lot of time myself." He peered down at his watch, which was cracked and broken. "I've only been in whatever this realm is—"

"Utenheim," Thor offered.

"Right, Utenheim, the End Realm, or what did Shango call it in our language? In Yoruba?"

"Ijọba Ipari," Shango offered.

"Right. Ijọba Ipari. It's only been, what, an hour or two since I've been here? Back on the Mortal Realm, we still have two months before Olokun comes to drown Eko Atlantic. I'm just worried if this," he pointed to his forehead, "will be okay. I already lost my memories the last time I crossed over. But I got some people I know back in the Mortal Realm who are... not all there, if you get my meaning."

"Don't worry yourself, mortal," Perun of the Slavics said, flipping his crimson cape over his shoulder. "Time works a bit differently here. You'll get back to your dimension without much time lost."

"You'll still suffer some memory loss though," Shango clarified. "Nothing can be done about that. Mortals are not meant to cross into the Planes while still being..."

"Alive?" Ayodeji asked.

"Right," Shango answered.

"That's good to know." Ayodeji nodded. "So you all have this Great War going on, huh?" He turned a curious expression on Shango. "Why isn't Oya with you then?—"

Just behind Shango, Lugh mimed zipping his lips to stop Ayodeji from continuing.

"She's one of the best warriors the Orishas have—"

Raijin and his animal companion jumped up and down to grab Ayodeji's attention.

"You shoulda seen her in the Sky Realm!—"

Perun, in his metal armor, tried his best to wave his hands without making a sound.

"And she wasn't even at full strength then. Imagine if she came here and—"

The gods slumped their shoulders in defeat, because in the next instant Shango left the table in a fury, leaving a wake of lightning bolts trailing at his heels. "Come, Lugh, let's patrol the perimeter for any Eaters."

"Say less, Commander," he said, bashful reds coloring his face.

"Hey! I see you catchin' on quick with the Earth-lingo, Lugh." Ayodeji perked up and gave the god a thumbs up, which was reciprocated. Too bad Shango wasn't as cheery or receptive.

Most of the other deities were called away on this duty or that. Soon there were only a handful left, with Ayodeji and Thor sitting alone at the grand round table.

"You know, if it is a favor you wish to ask of my friend," Thor started, "it's best *not* to bring up Oya. She's a touchy subject for him."

"Oh, yeah..." Ayodeji's eyes lingered over the tent flap Shango had retreated through. "The Ibeji—erm, the twin Orishas—they said something about the two of them gettin' into a big fight."

"More like a *gargantuan* fight, young mortal." Thor guzzled down a horn of ale.

"What happened?"

"Despite Oya being a touchy subject for Shango, he speaks about her all the time. Though I'm never allowed to ask follow-up questions. I just have to listen and keep quiet." Thor leaned in close enough for Ayodeji to smell the ale on his breath. "Never tell this to his other wives, Oshun or Oba, but Oya is his favorite by a fair few leagues. Shango has a bit of a reputation with the ladies, as I'm sure you know."

Ayodeji perked up. "That's where I get my swag from. My family says we have a direct bloodline to King Shango. We're truebloods."

"Yes, well... that same charm is what landed Shango in a hotbed of trouble. Well, a deliberate bit of trouble. He let it slip that he had been messing around. Just a small rumor... I think he mentioned using someone named Eshu to help him sell the fiction. Something about this Eshu transforming into a woman, if I recall correctly. I've done some of that pretending to be a woman stuff with Uncle Loki before as well, in fact. Funny how some of our stories overlap like that. Anyway, you can imagine all the fuss that caused if you've interacted with Oya at all. From how Shango tells it, she chased him around the Sky Realm with her machete, demanding his head on a spear and all that. It gave Shango the out he needed."

"I still don't get it." Ayodeji tried awkwardly to get his tiny human lips around his giant mug. He eventually decided on magically lifting the drink into his mouth instead. "Why would Shango get Oya mad like that?"

"You know the other name they call Oya, yes?"

"The Windweaver?"

"That as well. But Shango tells me she is also known as the bearded woman because she fights just as a man does. She was always the first to battle, side-to-side with her husband. And that is why Shango did what he did."

"Wouldn't he *want* her to be fightin', though? I mean, I never saw her fight at full power, but the storms she got goin' were ten times anything me and my friends could do."

"I don't know if you noticed, boy, but this whole thing," Thor swirled a finger to the stars peeking through the top of the tent, "is a suicide mission. It's written in the stars that my end will come here, in this war. A warrior's sacrifice. Same can be said for many others. If Oya would've joined us—"

"She'd get a first-class ticket to Valhalla." Ayodeji's shoulders slumped.

"I don't think it quite works that way for your Orishas," Thor quipped.

"Right... but, hey! When I showed up, it looked like you and Shango were taking out those shadows pretty easy. *And* you did it with each other's weapons."

"Heh, don't tell Shango, but it was damned difficult using those axes of his. They're too light. Not enough weight behind them. I was nearly hit more times than I would care to admit to him. But in all seriousness," Thor took another great swallow from his horn, "we are losing this war. It might not seem like it, but trust this old warrior; our defeat comes slow and long. The Eaters are ceaseless. Shango knows that better than most, so he did the one thing he knew would keep Oya away: he broke her heart."

"Damn..." Ayodeji held his hand over his mouth and rubbed at his nonexistent beard.

A brief silence rested between the mortal and the god until Thor tapped Ayodeji with his hammer. "So... tell me about this Marvelous Thor created by this Mr. Marvel. Sounds like *that's* the reason my power hasn't atrophied. What does he look like?"

That perked Ayodeji up. A little bit. "Heh, it's *Marvel's* Thor. A guy named Stan Lee and some other guys came up with him. And you two don't look alike at all, 'cept your hair. Well, your hair's got more of a reddish-blond going on in a certain light. And you kept calling Loki your uncle. In the Marvel movies, he's your brother, or half-brother or something."

"Hah! Uncle Loki! My brother?" Thor's boisterous laugh fell into a more somber tone. "Oh... how Uncle would have loved to hear that."

"And you don't have the same armor. But in the movies, he has this Old English vibe goin' on, and your accent is... Nordic, right?"

Thor nodded, then sighed. "Figures. If you leave a realm for as long as I have been gone, who can complain about accuracy, right?"

A few more deities entered the tent—one of them a giant bear who was missing a front leg, another, one of the revenants, who was missing an arm and an eye.

Ayodeji frowned. "I don't think I could enlist in a war if I knew I'd die. I mean, no one really does, right? Unless I get big mad at someone and don't even think of it. How do you do it, Thor? How do you let fate just say what you'll do and what you'll be?"

Thor cleared his throat and leaned in again. "Child, I'll let you in on a secret my old man told me when I was a boy: Fate can be made. It's not only meant to be followed."

"No Fate but what we make."

Thor gave the boy a faux frown. "Yes, this is a very good saying. It has a nice cadence to it."

"Ugh," Ayodeji groaned and smacked his head, "that wasn't me. That was my friend TJ. Some quote from this old movie with killer robots he watched all the time."

"The Mortal Realm had to deal with killer, er... what did you call them?"

"My guy, there's a whole lot I gotta explain to you," Ayodeji laughed, then eyed Thor with a tilted head. "You know, if you put on some shades, cut your hair short and dyed it darker, you'd look just like the Terminator. You're swole enough for it."

Thor leaned back in his chair with a thoughtful expression. "You remind me of him when I first met him, you know."

"Arnold Schwarzenegger?" Ayodeji flexed his tiny biceps. "I mean... I have been tryna hit the gym recently."

"No. Shango. He used to have that charisma you have. He's grown uptight these past centuries. I can only get him to break out of that wretched shell when we engage in battle." Amidst the growing clamor of the mess hall, Thor peeked over his shoulders before going on. "This might not work... but I'd like to give you something to take back to the Mortal Realm... I feel I am meant to."

Ayodeji perked up. "What is it?"

Thor waved his hand in the air, and a copper ring appeared between his large thumb and forefinger. A repeating runic symbol in the shape of an uppercase "N" or a slanted arch etched itself along the border. Each symbol glowed a fierce and bright blue. It was entirely majestic, and it clearly pulsated with great power. But there was one problem.

"I-is that a ring?" Ayodeji asked. "It looks more like a hula hoop."

"A hula hoop?"

Ayodeji waved it away. "Ah, more modern Mortal Realm stuff. I'm just saying that's way too big for me."

"Ah, yes. Never fear." Thor waved his hand again, and the ring floated toward Ayodeji. As it did, it reduced in size until it could fit into the tiny mortal's palm. The boy stared at it with awe.

"It's called the Lyn Ringe," Thor explained.

"Dope, dope..." Ayodeji's face scrunched up in confusion. "What does that mean?"

Thor chuckled. "It just means 'lightning ring.' Those symbols that are carved on the side are the runic symbol for the bull and storms. 'Uruz.' You're not one of my ancient children. So, hopefully, this ring will supply you with a lightning rune to help you in your battles to come."

"Oh, sick! I got a friend or two who study runic magic at this school named Greystone."

"Then those friends could guide you well." Thor cleared his throat. "Well, go on, try it on for size, see if it suits you."

"Yeah, yeah!" Ayodeji grabbed the ring and fit it around a finger on his left hand. A surge of electricity rushed through his body. The ring crackled with power, forcing his arm to spasm and jerk until a brilliant light filled the mess hall tent. A few revenants and deities in the mess hall shielded their eyes and complained about the light. When the radiance receded, a bolt of lightning cast from the ring skittered across the edge of Ayodeji's left eye. It left a single dark mark in the shape of the rune on the ring. Ayodeji didn't notice, but Thor eyed him closely.

"Sss, ouch." Ayodeji sucked in a harsh breath. He shook the ring and rubbed at the edge of his eye. "Damn, that stung."

Thor let out a full-bellied laugh. "Good! Good. It didn't kill you. Just marked you. You are a True Son of the Sky."

"This thing could've killed me!?" Ayodeji flung his hand away from himself as though the Lyn Ringe was contagious.

"Eh, only if you were lying about being a trueblood of Shango, then... it *might* have."

Ayodeji and Thor spent the next few hours talking about more oddities from the Mortal Realm until Thor, like the others, was called away to uphold his duties. Ayodeji waited in the mess hall until Shango returned with a band of war deities.

"Oh, look, Shango, your pet mortal is still here," Perun of the Slavic, with his winged helmet and long beard, laughed. "See if it wants a scratch behind the ear or a treat, would you? My wolves used to love that."

Shango seemed near to an eye roll and shoved Perun away. Ayodeji jumped from his seat and dashed in front of Shango before the Orisha could be served his offerings. "Hey! So before you fling me out into the stars again, I gotta tell you somethin'!"

"What?" Shango grunted so low and harshly it vibrated in Ayodeji's chest.

"So... Thor and I got to talkin'."

"He likes talking... unlike me."

"Really? Back on the Mortal Realm, you're supposed to be, like, the charmer of charmers. Did this God Eater War or whatever change you?" Shango shot violent eyes at him; Ayodeji threw up his hands in forfeit. "Yeah, yeah, I figured that much. But hear me out about Oya. You don't understand what's going on with her. I know you're only trying to protect her and—"

"Mind your words, child."

"Right... touchy subject." Then he mumbled, "Thor mentioned that. Listen, if you don't come back to the Mortal Realm with me *right now*, Oya is gonna end up gettin' herself killed. She's plannin' to throw hands with Olokun, Yemoja, Eshu, Olosa, the Ibeji, *and* maybe even Obatala... all on her own."

Shango waved him away and made his way to his offerings, which included a hill of red chicken and red peppers. "Obatala gave up his warriors' path when his destructive nature proved too great. He only deals in creation now. He'll be no issue for Oya."

Ayodeji vaulted onto a nearby table and jumped in front of Shango again. "But did you hear all the others I just said who'd be fighting her too? Olokun on his own is bad enough! And that's not even accountin' for Eshu's illusions *and* the Ibeji's sound magic. C'mon, you know she's in *way* over her head. If you care about her *for real*-for real, then you'll come back with me and fight." Ayodeji pierced Shango with a look over his glasses, appearing as a scrutinizing school teacher. "Unless... you think Olokun is too powerful for you."

Shango snarled at that. "Don't play with me, child. *I'm* the one who put him in those chains, to begin with."

Ayodeji threw up his hands again. "A'ight! A'ight! I'm just sayin'..."

"I can't just leave this place. The others need me." The mess hall had refilled with more deities. Blue and orange light flickered near the kitchen of offerings, where the lightning and fire gods gathered. "Thor needs me. It is not a question of choice. I must remain. It is both necessary and ordained. And we are all bound to the End Realm by magic greater than my own."

"Well..." Ayodeji grabbed a large bowl of yams that sparked with lightning. He had to hold it in two arms as he handed it to Shango. "Thor says Fate can be made, not just followed. Let's ask what he thinks."

12

When there was another lull in battle duties, Shango invited Thor to his tent at the behest of Ayodeji. Unlike Thor's space, which was relatively simple, Shango's tent was a bit more audacious, with every type of axe imaginable slung up on the walls. Near the foot of his bed sat a pot that Ayodeji had only heard stories of from the elders.

As Shango and Thor said their greetings by way of an arm wrestling contest, Ayodeji sauntered over to the pot. He dipped his nose over its rough iron rim. Inside, a huddle of storm clouds cascaded over bubbling liquid. This had to be the famous source of Shango's power. The same one Oya stole the first time she was invited into Shango's bed. When Oya had tasted only a mere drop from the pot, she gained a sliver of Shango's ability to lord over lightning.

What would happen if Ayodeji did the same? The Ashe pulsing from the pot practically called to him, seeped into his very pores. He sniffed, just to get an extra hint of the power hidden beneath. It didn't seem like a bad idea. Plus, he survived Thor's ring thingy.

"Get your nose out of that pot, child," Shango gruffed out. "Lest you want your insides to tear from the inside out. You seemed to barely survive getting to Ijọba Ipari to begin with. I suspect sampling from the sacred pot would kill you instantly."

Ayodeji took two quick steps away from the pot. He'd barely worked out how to use the lightning rune Thor had given him. No need to test the waters with Shango's pot on top of that. And the Orisha wasn't exactly wrong. Ayodeji nearly split himself in two trying to follow the Ashe line that led him to the End Realm.

"But I survived the trip, didn't I?" Ayodeji lifted his hand. "I mean, my family says we're truebloods. You're supposed to be my great, great, great, great grandfather times a hundred or whatever."

Shango twisted his fingers and the lid to his pot floated in mid-air, then slammed down to seal the thing shut. "Direct kin or not, keep away from my things before you break something."

"You should not shirk from your calling, brother," Thor said as he flexed his hand. He must've lost the arm wrestling contest. "The Norns of Destiny are often confusing, but they cannot be ignored, just as I can't ignore their prophecies about me. Clearly, they sent this boy to you. You are meant to return to the Mortal Realm once more. You said Anansi wrote them in the stars for you."

Shango made a fist. "The Fates spell of your doom. Forget them. They have been gone too long. I can hardly remember the last time I've seen my own. Orunmila is nothing but an echoed whisper in our ears."

"Don't be so hypocritical, friend. You favor the Fates, but only when the outcome is something you desire. Now that my Fate takes greater shape, you sing a different tune."

"We owe the Fates much, but we no longer need to answer to their call when they have gone quiet, if this mortal even *is* a call."

Ayodeji shrugged. "Beats me. All I know is that Oya said you were pulling me to you. Can't say nothin' about Orunmila. He definitely didn't send me."

"You see." Shango opened his palm to Ayodeji. "I've already denied the Mortal Realm time and time again. When Eshu came to me about the Trans-Saharan slave trade, I stayed by your side.

When Oshosi caught wind of that transatlantic business, I didn't budge. When we all heard about those World Wars, we all held our ground for the Great War. *This* war."

Thor lifted his hammer and pointed it at the mortal. "But this is different, brother. Those messengers were ethereal. This one is human. When's the last time we've had one of those cross into Utenheim? One that was living, of course. Hel, even the Eaters have a hard enough time getting here. Is that not enough of a sign?"

No immediate protest came from Shango's lips; the hesitation was all Thor needed.

"Don't give me that look," Shango bit. "And put away that smile, both of you."

Ayodeji thinned his grin into a tight line instantly. Thor, however, stayed his smile like it was carved into his beard permanently.

"You can't talk your way out of this calling," Thor said. "You must face this one head-on."

"Do you think I want to leave my people to their suffering?" Shango thumped his chest, genuine sorrow riddling his eyes. "Do you think hearing the stories from Eshu and Oshosi brings me joy? I fight here so that some of those children have a future. Not just the few I could potentially save from Olokun. We deities understand that better than all. That's why we are what we are. I'll be damned if I leave the Bolts compromised from the Great Enemy. You can't make me."

Thor's eyes darkened. "Oh, I very well can."

Ayodeji's chin jerked left and right between the two beings, his braids slapping his face with each turn. Were they going to fight? He saw what they did to their tents just off the back of them doing push-ups. Tension hung thick in the air, and Ayodeji swore he saw flickers of lightning cast from each of his heroes.

"Mortal," Thor said low and deep.

"Yes!" Ayodeji squeaked, clenching his butt for a combustion of fire and lightning. That sacred pot could protect him from any flying debris, couldn't it?

"Fetch me Aplu. He's usually hanging nearby. He's been looking for a promotion for ages. Laurel twigs are his crown, and he wields a staff of oak. Do you understand me?"

Ayodeji bounced nervously on his feet. "Yes, Ser Thor—erm—High General Thor."

"Then be off with you." Thor didn't break eye contact with Shango. "Now."

13

Ayodeji scurried away with the hop and speed of a tiny rabbit. Once his *pat-patting* receded in the distance, the sound of fists gripping leather handles took its place within the tent. Shango's corded forearms rested atop his knees. He squeezed his axe hilts with his hands. Thor's meaty hands sat atop his hammer. Electricity sparked between them. They sat like that, staring at each other for several moments, before Shango finally said, "What are you playing at, brother?"

"I'm pulling rank," Thor answered grimly.

Shango scowled. "Why?"

Thor lifted his hammer to the mouth of his tent. "I didn't realize it when we first met him, but this isn't the first time I've seen that child of yours. I told you when you tried to ignore me. I saw him in my dreams."

"You saw him in your dreams?"

"Seeing wouldn't be the right way of describing it. It's more how you describe the Ashe that stirs in your belly. And more than that... he survived the Lyn Ringe."

"Is that what he had around his finger? You could've killed the mortal."

"But I did not. And I knew I wouldn't. The Norns have made

that clear. And their messages would be clear to you as well if you had not locked away your heart all these eons. I understood why you have been doing it, trust me. It was the only way you could stop thinking about the mortals and your wife in the name of cold duty, more so than is healthy."

"I am plenty healthy." Shango waved him away. "Or did you forget the push-up contest we just had? Or that excuse for an arm-wrestling contest you just lost?"

"You know good and well I'm not talking about your physical health, brother. You've cut your heart off for so long and so well that you couldn't even recognize one of your own. That Ayodeji isn't just here to save his mortal friends from drowning. Don't you see it? He's here to save *you*, Shango."

Shango gritted his teeth, his jaw clenched. "How dare you? You know what I gave up. You know my resolve better than anyone else. You had your family with you when this started. I had nothing. No one."

"And I do not have them now, do I?"

"We Orisha are different, brother. Our ties to the Mortal Realm—to Earth—are deeply intertwined. We falter without Mother Nature's call, like a fish without water."

"And you have suffered without your water too long. *This* is how I will help *you*., By forcing you back into that pool, by commanding you as your High General to reconnect as you should have ages ago."

"If you believe this is something I should have done long ago, why command me now?"

"Because I'm the only one who would allow you to go back. I wouldn't even be able to convince Forseti. And... my time as your High General grows short..."

Shango blew out of his nose, low and deep. "And how would I return? There's no way out of the End Realm. Not even you, High General, can breach its borders. Did you plan to force Themis or the others on the Justice Council to let us use their fountain?"

Thor shook his head and walked over to a rune-carved chest of simple oak. He pulled out a rainbow shard that highlighted the edges of his pale skin. "This has at least one more use left in it for a round trip. I... must admit. In the early days, I kept it as an escape route—"

"A piece of the bifrost!? I thought that was destroyed when Loki and Heimdall—"

"It was. But I managed to salvage this fragment. And now I understand that it is meant for you. Use it, brother."

Shango stood hesitant, eyes fixed on the rainbow shard, uncertain of its power. He didn't want to leave Thor behind. Not because he feared the unknown and the uncertain dangers of Olokun and the Mortal Realm, but because he feared what waited for Thor in this one. What waited for all of them if the shadows got through for long enough. After Zeus had been swallowed up, they had seen some of their darkest days on his loss alone.

"You told me only deities and worthy beings could travel the bifrost," Shango finally managed to say.

"Seeing that boy survive the Lyn Ringe and making it all the way here on his own... you and I both know he's worthy. And Mjölnir let you use her. You both have the stuff."

"But I can't leave you on your own. Who will watch your back? Your estranged sons? Aplu? He barely has any power left in his reserves. No one can fight as well as me, especially when your nightmares have grown all the more—"

"Stop making excuses, Shango. I thought I made it clear this is not a debate."

Shango had half a mind to crush the bifrost shard between his fingers when the *pat-patting* of Ayodeji's feet returned.

"I found him! I found Aplu!" the boy's voice was muffled from the other side of the tent. "Don't kill each other yet!"

Ayodeji flung the tent flap aside and trotted in with Aplu, one of the ancients among the deities. Like most, he dwarfed the human, but where they contrasted in size, they were similar in the braids they wore atop their heads.

"You summoned me, High General?" he asked in a husky, aged voice.

"Yes, I did." Thor still didn't lift his gaze from Shango's. "I need you here as witness to my official order so that it may not be refused—"

"Do not do this, High General," Shango cut him off.

"Aplu will bare witness to my official order—"

"Friend, stay your tongue."

"This mission requires nuance so that the God Eaters are not tipped off—"

"*Brother*, I'm begging you."

"Shango is ordered by his *High General* to travel to Midgar along with his mortal to ensure Olokun does not have his way with the coast of his people." It was as though one of the black holes outside the tent had entered the space and evaporated all sense of sound and spirit. Shango didn't even look angry. He was absolutely stoic in what had to be a quiet inferno within.

"Be quick about it, General Shango." Thor stepped toward the exit. He lifted the tent flap and continued speaking over his shoulder. "We cannot manage the line too long without our hero."

"Can this testimony be corroborated with Aplu?" Themis in her high seat asked of Shango in the present time within the Court of All. Shango's mind had still been back in that dark tent, and the golden light of the courtroom made him squint.

Forseti of the Asgardians cleared his throat, his waist-length beard glowing with the room's radiance. "No, High Judge, it cannot. Aplu passed in the same battle as Thor did. That was one of our chief reasons for holding Shango as we are now. We've never had so many casualties at one time before."

"I can attest to that," Chaac of the Mayans added from the public benches. His battle axe and shield lay in his lap. "I was there just after Aplu fell, Esteemed Judges. He didn't have a chance with such a weakened position."

"It's the reason we did not bring it up, Esteemed Judges," Oshosi chimed in. "It would not be an admissible claim without corroborated evidence." He turned his hard jaw to Shango up on the stand. "As my charge knows well from our *many* conversations about the situation. Without Aplu, we have no way to verify Shango's claims."

That was another needle through Shango's heart. He had liked Aplu and all the wisdom he had imparted to them all. Now he was nothing but a dead god, like all of them soon would be.

"Esteemed Judges, if we may continue with the telling?" Oshosi offered, his feathered headdress seeming to droop along with his mood. "These are not easy memories for Brother Shango here to sift through."

A cloud of shame cast its shadow over Shango's thoughts as he recounted the moment he had obediently followed the order from Thor, despite his own reservations. The memory was a bitter medicine to swallow, an echo of a time when he had let his own convictions yield to another's will. As the next chapter of his narrative unfolded, he felt the weight of reluctant duty settle upon him, knowing that the story he had to reveal was far from the tale he wished to recount. But the undeniable truth had to come out to the Court of All.

14

Shango couldn't believe Thor would pull rank like that. Why would he put himself in danger for a band of mortals that didn't even worship him? Why compromise their position at the Andromeda Front when that giant serpent could pounce on him at any moment?

Anger boiled his blood, and he did his best to keep it all bottled within by concentrating on the lightning tunnel he generated before him. Rainbow sparks scattered about him and his axes as he struck the bifrost he used as a flint to hold the portal door open.

The bifrost was strong. It did well to start up the magic Shango needed to jump from the End Realm to the Mortal Realm. But it was like using an almost-spent flint against a dull blade with a damp husk. It burned eventually, just not after a lot of very hard work to light a spark.

"It's okay, Shango." Ayodeji stood a safe distance away from the deity, behind a pillar of space rock that seemed sturdy enough to withstand Shango's ire. It had been several hours since Shango had started to craft the portal. The longer it took him to manifest it, the more anger that seemed to cast off his shoulders in waves of bolts. "Thor will be all right. He said there was a time he fought without you."

Shango spun on the mortal boy with heat. "That's when he had Zeus and Marduk and many other powerful allies at his side. These times are different."

Ayodeji sank into himself, his back pressed into stone. They stood atop the Crescent Moon Rock—the same place where Ayodeji had shown himself from the start. It made the most sense for Shango to make his portal here since he figured it had some sort of spiritual significance. At least, that's what his Ashe had told him. And he always trusted in his Ashe.

"This wouldn't have happened if you weren't here," Shango huffed. Then, with an almost annoyed voice, he said, "How did a simple mortal like you breach the protective enchantment of Ijọba Ipari? Not even the God Eaters can do that." Shango stopped his sparking for a moment to listen to the mortal's answer.

"I-it's like I told you, Orisha Shango." Ayodeji bowed his head, his braids falling with him. "My friend TJ Young got these special powers. Like... he just makes everything more powerful, makes Ashe flow easier. He's probably why I'm alive right now. If you want to know how to cross the realms, that's your guy."

"Hmmm." Shango considered Ayodeji's words a moment before going back to his work. Rainbow light flashed across his face again as he said, "I've not heard of such power since the Great Monarch Olodumare. I would like to meet this TJ Young."

Ayodeji—perhaps feeling comfortable after Shango said words to him that weren't being shouted or grunted—withdrew from his rock pillar's protection. He ventured a few feet from Shango to observe his handiwork. But when he drew too close, Shango repositioned his body to block his view.

"My bad, my bad!" Ayodeji took a few steps back, but not so far as his original hiding place. "So... sounded like the Fates got y'all all spooked back there. What's that all about?"

"We worked together at first—we war deities and the Fates. Until recently, for example, we had a defense built on the sacrifice of the Mayan pantheon. A large piece of the great seal that would not have been possible if not for the Fates' foresight and intervention. But the time of that seal has passed, and relations with the Fates strained long ago..." Shango swallowed and didn't continue right away.

"What happened?"

"I don't know all of it. The Fates had broken away just as I first joined the fight. The Battalion even had me try to seek out our Fate, Orunmila. But He Who Knows the Stars did not want to be found. Could be gone like most of us, for all I know."

Shango rubbed out one last spark that blossomed into a rainbow flame and roared true as a streak of lightning. He wiped sweat from his brow as his portal opened up at last. Then he waved a hand for Ayodeji to step inside. The boy obliged, his feet lifting from the ground as he fell into the lightning tunnel he had become familiar with only a day before. He drifted forward from left to right as he ran his hand along the lightning wall. It was easier to get through than the tunnel he used to get to Shango. Made sense. Shango would be a professional at this sort of thing. Ayodeji was just wandering through the dark when he belched out his lightning shaft.

When Shango caught up to him, soaring just at his side, Ayodeji spoke once more. "There was a story at camp about that. About how Orunmila gave the ancestors one message, a prediction of the Unseen Monarch's return. That's Olodumare, right? The top of the top of the Orishas?"

Shango nodded simply.

"The exact details of Orunmila's message are still up in the air among us diviners and the elders," Ayodeji continued. "But apparently one thing the oracles all agree on is the birth of a Promised Child who would 'uncover the Unseen Monarch.' Do you know anything about that?"

"Yes, I know a little about it. Nothing about a Promised Child, though. Just that the Great Monarch told us all we were splitting off from the mortals. Then he went off to whatever Plane he's on now, doing whatever work he's doing, using that all-knowing mind of his. I try to stay out of all that oracle work and star-reading. Much easier to vanquish shadows than debate constellations."

"I guess that's where I take after Ogun more. I like figuring stuff like this out."

"I thought you claimed to be trueborn?"

"That's what all my family says. But Oracle Ruby says I've got more Ogun in me than my family lets on. But I like what Thor was saying about us making our own Fate and all that. It might be different with you deities, though. I mean, your Fates are different from our oracles. I'm sure they get it more right than ours does. Our Promised Child was supposed to be this girl named Ifedayo Young, but she got killed and the 'Unseen Monarch' hasn't been uncovered. So... clearly, that was wrong, huh? But that didn't stop my friend from fighting for her memory."

"This TJ Young you've mentioned?"

"Yup. One and the same. That's my boy right there. Didn't like him at first. We actually threw hands at one point. But we all good now."

"Heh, I had a similar introduction to Thor." It was the first chuckle Ayodeji had heard from his Orisha. So the good ol' Shango he knew from the stories was in there. Somewhere.

"All I'm sayin' is that Fate can be changed, Shango. TJ is living proof of that. Even Thor's fate that he's so afraid of can be changed. I think he believes that, too."

Shango frowned at that last part. *So like Thor. To give hope where he has none for himself.*

The lightning portal around them began to fracture, like a concussive force shot its way through the hull of a spaceship. All the air was getting sucked out. The vacuum captured Ayodeji first. The boy shouted and flung his tiny hands to grab onto something, but there was nothing to clutch. Shango outstretched a hand, but was too slow and the boy was too small.

How was his lightning tunnel penetrated? Was Thor's bifrost too weak to handle the trip? They were well away from any God

Eaters. Those shadows couldn't compromise his tunnel when they were locked up so far away in the End Realm. Before questioning further, Shango dove into the fracture in his tunnel. He shot out into an endless starfield. An ordinary starfield, free of any gas clouds.

"Shango, over here!" Ayodeji shouted from between the stars where he floated. He was pointing up above. "Look! Shooting stars. Shooting stars everywhere."

Shooting stars streaked across the sky like fireworks, leaving trails of light in their wake. It was not often Shango felt small and insignificant in a sea of stars. At this point, he had spent most of his years among them. Yet at that moment, somehow, the starfield before him felt grand, mesmerizing.

Wait.

It wasn't *just* shooting stars. It was a code! An ancient code Shango hadn't seen since before the Great Separation. A message that had recently dominated his dreams.

The shooting stars grew and terminated in specific webs of information. But it was written in a language Shango barely remembered. A language lost to time, he thought.

Wait... a web of information?

Was that... Anansi?

"There's so many!" Ayodeji said in awe. "Is it always like this 'round here?"

"No, it's a message from one of the Fates."

"For real!? But you said—"

"Yes, I said they don't talk to us anymore."

"So, who's trying to talk to us now?"

"A close cousin. Anansi."

"From Ghana? From the Akan people?" Ayodeji had studied Anansi in his summer camps. He'd always been interested in a deity that lorded over stories themselves. In fact, he had a desire to minor in the deity when he went off to university in a few years, but his father had turned his nose up at the notion. Trueblood pride and all that.

"We only look to Shango," his father had told him time and time again. *"If we look too much to others, even other Orishas, we will sully our bloodline, our True Ashe."*

"The Spider, yes," Shango confirmed. "He's weaving us a story now with these shooting stars. I just can't decipher his message. I never had a mind for these tricks."

"Do you think he's able to get through to you because we're outside Ijọba Ipari's shield?"

"Maybe... that would make sense."

"All right, let's try to figure out what he's saying." Ayodeji floated from left to right as he noted each passing of a star. "Oracle Ruby was teaching us how to read the stars. I developed an app to process all this stuff. Got the idea from her, actually. She's really smart, by the way. I think you would—"

"Boy, keep focus before the message passes."

"Oh, right! Sorry."

Ayodeji gazed up at the starry sky, trying to make sense of the cryptic message. Anansi's web was woven intricately, but he spent the time necessary to crack it, going through logical deductions that admittedly impressed Shango. Apparently, this Oracle Ruby had taught the boy well.

"Ah-hah!" Ayodeji threw a single finger up in the air. "Wait. That can't be right."

"What? What does Anansi say?"

Ayodeji turned from the stars and stared at Shango with a bewildered expression. "He says... 'Forgive me, cousin.'"

15

The members of the Court of All sat forward in their seats now, doing away with almost all their previous decorum. Previously shadowed faces leaned forward to gleam with the golden light blanketing the courtroom. Tight chests loosened with curiosity. None more so than Oshosi.

"You see, it's just as I said, Esteemed Judges!" Oshosi clapped his hands together with glee. Clearly, he must've thought Shango had come to his senses telling them about his encounter with the Lord of Story. "Anansi knocked Shango off course and compromised Shango's ability to return to the End Realm."

"But you failed to mention that Shango was on his way back to one of your Orisha Planes and the Mortal Realm." Modi was red in the face again. It was hard to tell where his beard ended and where his skin began.

"Esteemed Judges," said his brother, whose beet-red skin contrasted starkly against his blond hair, "I demand Shango to be thrown back in his cell immediately. He compromised the borders of Utenheim and can do it again with whatever power he—"

"I told you the bifrost is gone," Shango gritted. "All of it. And I have no interest in going back at this time. The issue with Olokun is resolved. My people are safe. Right now," he tapped the marble stand before him, "I need to be out on the front lines like I was before. My wife, Oya, can make up the difference for Thor."

Modi scoffed; Oya, arms crossed tightly around her chest, scowled back at the Asgardian.

"We should invoke the Channeling against Shango now," Modi demanded. "Shango was loyal to Utenheim until his woman got involved. If another of his lovers cries for his help—"

"Again," Oya rolled her neck, "not his lover, his *wife*—"

"He could put us in a precarious situation again. And this time it could be our Esteemed Judges who will be jeopardized."

"The front line will be jeopardized if you strip me of my essence with the Channeling," Shango said.

Magni grunted at his brother's side. "Do not fret, Esteemed Judges. My brother and I will put that power to good use once the Bolts reabsorbed Shango's energy."

Themis lifted a single graceful hand. "I would like to hear more from Shango's story. This is our first report of a Fate in far too long."

"Yes," Mithra added, their crimson robes rustling with their lean. "What did Anansi mean by 'forgive me'?"

Shango took a deep breath and clenched his fists. He attempted to steady himself as he prepared to speak the rest of the whole truth. Memories of what came next flooded his mind, forcing his heart into a frenzy and his palms to sweat.

"I didn't think of it then," he said. "I couldn't have known at the time. But he was asking me forgiveness for what would happen... to Thor."

"Why is Anansi asking for forgiveness?" Ayodeji questioned.

Shango stared up at the starfield in confusion, searching for meaning in the jumble of stars. Surely the mortal boy got the translation incorrect. As far as Shango was concerned, there was nothing Anansi needed forgiveness for, except for going off on his own path with his mysterious cohorts. Except for what they were doing right then and there...

Revelation raced through Shango. "The Great Separation was proposed by the Fates initially, or so I've been told. They always wanted us far away from the mortals. But they wouldn't tell us why. Or *couldn't* tell us. I still don't understand how their magic works. It wasn't until we realized what the God Eaters were that we understood it. When Zeus was lost to their Shadow Realm."

"So... he's saying sorry for not being able to warn you about Zeus?"

"No, he's asking for forgiveness because he's trying to stop us from getting back to our people on the Mortal Realm." Shango snatched Ayodeji up in his hand and rushed for his lightning tunnel that still raced across the stars. "Come. We should be okay. Anansi gave us that riddle in the stars to kill time. He's going to let Olokun drown that coast, but we could not have lost more than a day or two."

When they dipped back into the portal, they were no longer headed for the deep waters of the Aqua Realm. Through the fractures of lightning bolts and rainbow sparks, clouds peppered through. The path to the Sky Realm.

"No! He's diverted us from the Aqua Realm," Shango seethed. "Could we get to your friend through the Sky Realm?"

"Maybe?" Ayodeji shrugged. "I can show you the way we came in from the golden chain."

But when they got to the end of the portal they were met with a veiled archway. The translucent curtain bore a note, the ink etched on it wavy, almost whimsical. It read:

Stitching the mystical curtain. Please come back after my lunch break.

—Eshu

"Ah, Gatekeeper, you wretched fool!" Shango bit out as he led Ayodeji to another entrance. They followed the lightning path until it darkened. Through the crackling funnel, the crust of lava and earth sizzled until they reached a circular threshold of fire and earth. This time, written in the lava rock that shone bright against fiery rock, a message read:

This door needs a little more time to prepare.
Check directions for pre-heating instructions.
—Eshu

"Oh, man," Ayodeji complained. "I really hate tricksters."

"You and me both, child. Come."

And back they went into the lightning portal. They traveled a short distance until a spotlight manifested at the end of the tunnel. As it grew larger, it took on the hue of a light blue, like looking through the viewport of a submarine. They had a straight shot to the Aqua Realm. But as their momentum took them forward, that blue light did not grow larger to accommodate their size as it should have. Instead, Shango had to slow their speed before they crashed headfirst into the glass. And it was a good thing he did. That blue light that appeared as a viewport was more than figurative. The lightning tunnel led to nothing but a window pane. And little letters were written across the glass:

Out for repairs. Be back soon.
—Eshu

"The Gatekeeper has us locked out *again*!" Shango sneered, pressing one eye through the viewport. Only the bottom of a kelp field revealed itself beyond. "Wretched trickster. I never liked that fool. Olodumare should have never given him so many thresholds to watch over."

"That's why none of you Orishas come to see us diviners no more, huh?" Ayodeji asked as he tapped the glass. "How long will this charm last?"

"Hard to say. I haven't seen Eshu in a while. Not sure where his Ashe is these days. We'll have to wait until this enchantment weakens. He was expecting us; he was expecting *me*." Shango touched the side of his tunnel and allowed lightning to funnel through his body. To Ayodeji, it seemed like he was fixing to blast the window pane and shatter it to pieces. How long would it take for him to channel enough energy to get through, though?

"Wait." Ayodeji pressed his face into the window pane. "Wait, wait. I think that's TJ."

Just past the field of kelp, the figure of a boy stood at the bottom of the ocean. He spun on his heel with wild eyes, swiping at unseen ghosts.

"What's he doing?" Shango asked.

"I don't know. He's a weird guy, but not *that* weird. He must've got out of the Sky Realm and made it here." Ayodeji pounded on the glass. "TJ!" The TJ boy stopped clutching at his head and looked over his shoulders. Ayodeji pounded the glass again. "TJ!" This time, the boy was able to find the source of his friend's words. "TJ, we've been looking all over for you! Eshu locked us out of the Aqua Realm!"

"I don't understand," Shango said. "What can your mortal friend do to help us?"

"Like I told you, he's got special powers. He ain't really a mortal. He's... something else. At least that's what you Orishas keep saying about him. Give me a second. He seems a little stressed out. Let me give him a pep talk."

The boy *did* look delirious and a little thinner than a human male his size should've been. Was food scarce in the Mortal Realm these days? And what about those bags and dark shadows under his eyes? Those features were usually reserved for elders.

"The glass, TJ! Touch the glass! You're the key to breaking it!"

The boy named TJ made slow movements to the viewport. It seemed like it took a great effort for him to move at all. He held a wooden staff in his hand with a double helix at its center. When he pulled one of his hands away from it, it was like watching a sloth let go of a branch and reach out for fruit. Eventually, the boy's finger met the surface of the glass, and it was as though a latch unlocked deep within Shango's very Ashe. Perhaps the mortals in the old world were more impressive than Shango originally thought.

At least this TJ boy was extraordinary.

Ayodeji must've felt the unlocking of Ashe too, because he said, "Good." And the glass began to crack. "Now get down."

"Huh?" the boy named TJ tilted his head in question.

Ayodeji drifted away from the window. "You're up, big guy! Do your worst."

Shango nodded and approached the cracking window, where the water was already leaking through. He got himself level with the glass, lifted his axes, and caught sight of the TJ boy. The mortal's mouth fell open and his eyes shot wide.

"He said get down, child." Shango lifted his axes overhead and generated lightning from the entirety of his tunnel. Then he shot their energy forward and blasted through the barrier Eshu had created. TJ ducked out of the way and water poured in around Shango and Ayodeji. Waves tried to force Shango back, but he was stronger. He pressed his magical weight into the raging waters and forced his way into the Aqua Realm.

"Stay right behind me, Ayodeji," he commanded. "Or you'll get swept away."

In an instant, Shango took in the whole of his surroundings. Below was the TJ boy among the kelp fields; ahead was Eshu wielding a staff that pulsated with power it shouldn't have held. Ayodeji was right. The Ashe of several Orisha were trapped within Eshu's crystal.

That needed to change.

Shango felt his eyes blaze like underwater stars. He summoned crackling bolts of lightning that danced among the seaweed. Eshu weaved through the water, attempting to throw cloned illusions about him. It was a poor attempt at concealing his moves. Today, his tricks seemed feeble. The image of his illusions fractured, making it easy for Shango to decipher the true Eshu among the waves.

Shango shocked the illusions into nothingness, then hurled fireballs that lit up the underwater realm. Eshu's illusions wavered, and he darted away just in time, his usual laughter replaced with yelps.

In truth, Eshu had never been Shango's match. But today, he was even weaker, struggling to keep up with Shango's elemental onslaught. What had drained the usually crafty Orisha of his strength?

An idea crackled in Shango's mind, and he turned his eyes upward, where the Mortal Realm lay. Eshu had been the center of a massive ritual, one aimed at lifting tidal waves against the human structures that stretched high in the clouds.

No wonder Eshu was drained. Such a feat required immense energy, and the underwater battle was just a small portion of that cost.

Seizing the moment, Shango gathered his power, a storm of thunder and fire swirling around him. Eshu's eyes widened, realizing he was trapped, his illusions now fading like the last light of day.

Shango's voice echoed through the water. "It's over, Eshu. Your illusions can't save you now."

Sustaining his crimson blast, Shango directed its energy directly into the center of the crystal lodged in Eshu's staff. As soon as his electric bolts made contact, the crystal began to crack like a fragile egg. The fissures gave way to new energy that stuck to the air, like opening a door to a fresh new day. Energy filled Shango like he had not felt in ages: the gentle winds of Obatala, the carefree sense of childhood from the Ibeji twins, the salty brine of Olosa, and more.

"Olokun! Yemoja!" the Trickster cried out through gnashed teeth, the grip on his staff shaking violently. "He is here! Shango is here! The Hero is back!"

16

In the far watery distance, two shadows arose. They twisted to Eshu's cries for help, and, with their turn, came the stink of Shango's old foe: Olokun, Yemoja at his side. It was surprising Yemoja was with him. Usually, she would be reeling him in during a time like this, telling him to make peace where he would've sought war. Both stood tall, despite them being a great distance away.

A crown plastered with seashells, starfish, and clams surrounded Yemoja's head. Her hair was long and matted with tiny beads, bells, and coral embedded in each lock of hair, which covered her bare chest. The beaded necklace that fell from her neck hung low near her belly, where the beginning of a huge tail fin brushed against the tallest of the kelp below.

Large and stoic as ever was Olokun, with sweeping long hair that drifted over his shoulders. Obsidian skin cascaded over bulging muscles, with an outfit that barely hid any of his lean physique.

Shango gave a quick glance to the waves above, where the Mortal Realm lay. He could barely make out large metal structures with thousands of squared bright eyes that swayed to and fro. Some of them crashed into the ocean with substantial force.

He and Ayodeji were too late.

The drowning of Lagos, Nigeria—the old Oyo Empire—had already begun.

"Hurry, TJ!" Shango heard Ayodeji shout from somewhere behind. Olokun and Yemoja made their fast approach from across the ocean floor. "Help Shango. You gotta bust those Orishas out!"

"Right!" TJ answered, and he swam to Shango's side.

Ayodeji spoke true. The mortal, TJ, was something different... a hybrid of an ordinary human and an extraordinary deity. The boy's Ashe felt bright, like the center of a star. Despite him being as small as a human, his energy filled Shango with the strength of a thousand storm clouds.

Not even with Thor at this side did Shango feel as powerful.

Olokun and Yemoja ripped through the current straight for them. They came at them with the speed of a spear thrown by Lugh of the Celtics himself. At their backs, a horde of sea creatures pressed forward in their wake, a thousand eyes radiating with violence. Sharks. Octopi. Olokun even seemed to convince a few hundred merpeople out of hiding to aid him. Ayodeji came to Shango's other side, opposite TJ. He flung out bolt after bolt toward Olokun and Yemoja from his fingertips. His added boost was but a drip in the pool of Shango's elevated power via TJ, but the mortal was trying, at least.

"Ugh!" TJ groaned. Shango gave him a quick glance. The boy's eyes were glowing white, not unlike a deity's would at full strength. And somehow, the boy was not already dead from the use of the magic. Proof that he was no mere mortal. But that sheer show of power was short-lived. The same white light that filled the boy's eyes ripped through his arms. The well of Ashe he sourced from was too deep for his feeble mortal body. Even the staff in his hands started to splinter and crack into pieces.

Am I killing the boy?

With more power than Shango had even known he could be filled with, he severed his ties with TJ and held onto what was given. He roared, lifting his axes overhead and bringing down a deluge of lightning. The crystal in Eshu's staff exploded into pieces—so thoroughly obliterated that the remains were nothing but sand drifting in the ocean waters. And with it, the Orisha spirits were free. First to exit was Obatala with his pale skin and shaved head, then the twins with their child-like faces, and still more.

As the dust continued to settle, Olokun and Yemoja came within yards of Shango. Big mistake.

With the power that had been building up between him and TJ, he flung out another volley of lightning that struck Olokun directly in his chest.

"Ugh!" the Orisha barked in anguish. Olokun had never done well against Shango's lightning, a natural weakness to Olokun's water magic. A form of checks and balances designed by the Great Monarch himself. But the anguish didn't just stop with Olokun. Shango's lightning linked from the leader to his partner and all their minions in a daisy chain that must've stretched for leagues upon leagues. The scene was a grouping of spasming figures, both small and large.

"Obatala, hurry and get the young mortals!" one of the Ibeji twins, Kehinde in blue cloth, shouted.

The other, Taiwo in red cloth, added in a rhyme, "Grab them and send them through the portal!"

They had gotten through the Aqua Realm, but that still left the crossover into the Mortal Realm above, where the true destruction was being wrought. Pockets of fire bloomed above the ocean ceiling.

"I've got them!" came the gentle voice of Obatala, who wore his signature white robes. "Olosa, calm those waves on the other side. Another one of those skyscrapers is coming down."

A giant woman who appeared half-fish glided upward. "Already on it!"

Had he not been holding back Olokun and his armies, Shango would've smiled seeing all his brothers and sisters working together.

Shango poured more lightning into the link that funneled through Olokun's chest until the Orisha finally called for a retreat. It wasn't until Shango was sure Olokun and his group had sunk into the shadows that he turned his attention upward, to where a new set of tidal waves raged.

Bursting through the Plane of the Aqua Realm, he entered the Mortal Realm as an *actual* streak of lightning. The sensation was almost too overwhelming. A million voices and prayers called out to Shango. He had received them before in Ijọba Ipari, but merely as whispers. Echoes. Now, with the Mortal Realm's energy slapping him across the face like a morning-time strike from Thor, Shango realized he hadn't properly breathed in ages.

Now, his spirits were fully recharged.

Shango's eyes widened as he surveyed the nightmarish tableau that stretched before him. The once serene coastline was now a battleground of chaos and destruction. The metal towers, once proud monuments of human ingenuity, were toppling like giants. Except for a single tall statue of Olokun at its center.

Explosions rocked the air, painted the sky with fiery bursts that competed with the night stars. The anguished cries of mortals mingled with the eerie howl of the wind. Yet amidst the apocalyptic scene, a few towers stood tall, their defiant silhouettes etched against the tumultuous sky.

Determination ignited in Shango's eyes; he was a guardian of this land, these people. He needed to end this horror.

Following the line of his red lightning through the stormy sky, he watched as Olosa manifested as waves in the Mortal Realm. Her great waters counteracted a tidal surge that thrashed against the metal fortresses. The "skyscrapers" as Obatala had called them. To the side, near the beach, Obatala—appearing as a cloud —dropped the mortal boys on the sands. And up in the sky where the winds roiled the strongest... was Oya.

Shango set his path for her.

As the sky darkened, metal creaked, and thunder roared, Shango in his red-lightning form dove into the essence of Oya's storm. Oya was deep in her battlemind and must've thought the surge of energy Shango filled her with was a second—or perhaps third or fourth—wind. She used his energy and shot red lightning out against a tidal wave. Upon impact, the ocean waters burst into harmless mist.

Shango grinned as he watched her work. She was perfect. Absolutely perfect. She moved with impeccable form, her lightning strikes powerful and precise, her wind blasts strong and widespread. Her stamina never faltered. She never used more energy than was necessary. Yet she never pulled back either. A perfect economy of motion. No wasted movement. Techniques Shango had never taught her.

A style all her own.

He knew he had found the perfect partner, both in battle and in life. How could he ever leave her to the Mortal Realm to waste? How could he never give her the choice to fight in concert with him? With her at his side against the God Eaters, perhaps there was some hope for the failing warfront.

He couldn't wait to introduce her to Thor.

"Oya," he said gently, softly. He announced himself only when she wasn't actively breaking up a wave. "Merge with me fully. Let us be done with Olokun as we have been done with him before."

As expected, Oya stopped cold. Her essence calmed briefly. Then she said, with a bitter rage that brought another smile to Shango's face, "Took you long enough, òlòṣí."

With a crack of lightning, Shango and Oya merged. Their powers intertwined and strengthened. The wind picked up, whipping sand and seawater into a frenzy. Bolts of lightning struck Olokun's waves, forcing them to tremble and retreat.

With a deafening roar, Olokun emerged from the ocean in one last effort. He towered over the mortals on the beach as an impossibly gigantic wave. But the lightning and wind were too much for him to handle, Shango could *actively* feel it.

The Orisha was weak. So very weak.

With a final burst of energy, Shango and Oya struck Olokun with a powerful bolt of lightning and wind, driving him back into the ocean, back into the Aqua Realm, saving thousands of lives.

The oceans settled back into a normal, ordinary flow. Shango surveyed the damage that was left to the coast. No wonder Olokun and Yemoja were so weak. They had to stir up enough Ashe to lay waste to dozens of those metal dwellings—skyscrapers, Obatala had called them.

A sharp wind-slap swiped across Shango's lightning shaft.

"How dare you do that to me, Shango!" Oya bellowed, then revved up for another slap. This time with her lightning-whip that trailed through the skies. Shango caught it in his own lightning shaft. Then, suddenly, clouds manifested around his form. Clouds sprouted forth from his very spirit, generating a single drop of rain that fell on the wreckage far below.

"What?" Oya gasped. Her next response came out low, as though she didn't want any other mystical forces listening in. "Since... since when do you cry?"

Shango wouldn't have called it crying. It was a single drop of rain that escaped him, but he would not argue the point. Instead, he confessed. "I... I was such a fool. *Am* such a fool. Your beauty today. On the battlefield. It was... inspiring. Touching, even."

Oya's cloud-form lit with pockets of lightning. Shango remembered this to mean she was giving him a look. And without warning, a gust of tumultuous wind came hard across Shango's lightning bolt. White heat entered his essence, the pain of Oya's wind-slap only making him all the more proud. She hadn't lost *any* of her fire. Not a single ember.

"I deserved that," Shango confessed.

Her first strike had been a mere reaction, a half measure. This second one was concentrated, aimed to do damage. But her next words struck even harsher.

"I thought you cared..."

Devastated, Shango peered into her clouds with melancholy. He never thought his actions would have had such an effect on

Oya. Part of him thought she would have moved on. But he had done real harm, more harm than any of his greatest lightning bolts or axe strikes could have ever doled out.

So, with the speed of a comet, Shango entered Oya's storm clouds, filling her spirit with his own. In mortal-form this would've been something like a kiss. One that was deep, and long, and angry, and fiercely genuine.

"Tell me that kiss was from someone who doesn't care, my love."

Oya's clouds trembled. Slightly. "N-not fair. You can't use those bolts on me and get away with—"

Shango lightning-kissed her again. Between the pulsations of loving energy, Oya sneered. "Oh, I hate you so much."

"You make me crazy, too. You don't even know. And empty words aren't enough to make up for what I've done to you. So I can only do better from here on out. I *will* do better by you. And I will never leave you again. That... is a husband's promise."

"You had better never... *ever* leave me alone in this world again." She wrapped her clouds around him as she thrashed his back with wind. To the mortals below, it would've looked like gusts of air roiling about a streak of red lightning. "What took you so long, you wretched fool?"

"What do you mean? It's only been a few days."

"It's been two moons since those mortals freed me from Eshu's staff."

"Moons?" Shango drew back from Oya to read her winds. She was serious. Her angry tears manifesting as rain spoke the truth of it.

Then it dawned on Shango. *That bastard Anansi!*

He didn't just make them lose time getting back to the Mortal Realm, he made them lose time getting back to the End Realm. That was supposed to be impossible. Ijọba Ipari sat outside of space and time.

But the Fates, like always, had a way of subverting the impossible.

That's what Anansi's message had meant. Not a cry for forgiveness for something in the distant past or a delay getting to the Mortal Realm, but a plea for what was about to befall Thor. If Shango had lost two moons in the Mortal Realm, he didn't want to think what could've been lost in the End Realm. That was a calculation for a deity much smarter than him. All he needed to know was that he needed to be long gone from this place.

Shango wrapped his bolt around the edge of Oya's storm. He generated a portal with the morsel of the bifrost he had left.

"I told you I'd never leave you again, so..." Shango took in a deep breath. "Let me show you where I've been all these ages."

"But what about the mortals?" The change in Oya's clouds made it look like she was quirking an eyebrow at Shango.

"They'll be fine now that Olokun is gone and licking his wounds. My brother needs us now. He's in danger."

"You have a brother? Since when?"

"Not a blood brother. A brother-in-arms. So many have been lost already. Marduk. Zeus."

"Zeus!? The Zeus? He's been missing too, according to the Greek pantheon. What have you fools been up to?"

"Let me show you. We have to go. Now!"

17

Outside one of the tall courtroom windows, a streak of lightning struck across the cosmic heavens. It reminded Shango of how fast and desperate he was to get back to Thor after realizing Anansi's deceit. Shango grunted low at the witness stand. He should've seen it coming. He had spent all those ages rubbing shoulders with Eshu and his troublesome tricks. Back in their heyday, Eshu and Anansi got along like first cousins. Stars, they practically were first cousins. And if not for the Great Monarch ordering Eshu to overwatch the Mortal Realm, Shango was sure the Trickster would've been in league with the Spider.

"You're not going to leave out the most tragic part, are you, cousin?" someone said from the public benches. Between the corpse-like cloaks of the four horsemen sat an ordinary-looking man of middle age. He wore a three-piece suit of purple. White stripes in the shape of a spider's web were stitched into the fabric. A perfect compliment to his umber skin.

The signature look of Anansi the Spider.

Shango clenched a fist against his witness stand. The Spider had a lot to answer for.

"If the court is willing to hear a story," Anansi said. "I would wish to share it."

Everyone in the courtroom was ghost quiet—except for Themis. "How are you here?" The brow over her blindfold betrayed no emotion.

"We were told a great curse would befall any Fate that communicated directly with us," the red-headed Modi added, his jaw slacking. His brother, Magni, was just as shocked as he.

"Oh, that's still very much the case," Anansi assured him as he pressed his hands into his suit. "This... will be my last story. The divine enchantments surrounding this Holy Courtroom will protect me for an extended time, but not long. Else I'd be nothing but a husk already. So I'll promise to keep it short."

Magni whipped to the high podium. "Esteemed Judges, we cannot interrupt this case, even for a Fate. We must subject Shango to the Channeling or—"

Themis lifted a slow hand to silence the Asgardian. She turned her blindfold to Anansi, indicating he could go on.

Anansi lifted up on his bench, brushing shoulders with the horsemen. He excused himself of the bump, dusted off his purple threads, and scooted to the central golden fountain.

A collection of staccato gasps filtered through the public benches. The air hummed with energy as all eyes fixed upon the unexpected figure stepping into the sacred spotlight. Anansi, the legendary Father of Story, seemingly re-emerged from the annals of time, weaved his way through the sea of divine beings. Whispers of disbelief spread quickly, and some gods kneeled in reverence. Tears welled in the eyes of a few, witnessing the return of a deity long thought to be a myth. The courtroom of gods had borne witness to countless tales, yet none could compare to this unprecedented moment.

As the crowd continued to stir, Anansi ran his hand through the flowing fountain water. He admired it as though he were a desert wanderer discovering water for the very first time. Or perhaps someone appreciating something that would soon be lost.

"You know," he finally said, and the crowd quieted, "the flow of time isn't some straight line, as the mortals or even some of us deities would believe. Yes, it's true that time is an ever-flowing stream that moves forward at a constant rate. That can never be changed. The possibilities of that flow can be dammed, redirected, but never, ever stopped. And each time this Divine Council gets in the way of the Fates, the flow of that stream falls outside of our control furthermore. What's important to know is that we must be the Shepherds of the Stream. If our hold of the flow is stopped, the God Eaters will snatch it away from us like a parent to bickering children. Thor was always going to leave us, but Aplu and all the others we lost these past few days could have been avoided. Their demises are a result of the weakening flow. A sacrifice to Time to earn us more in this eleventh hour."

Shango scowled. "What do you know of sacrifice, cousin?" As far as he was concerned, Anansi was more at fault for Thor than anyone here. Though it was true they all denied signs from the Fates. Deliberately.

"Oh, to be sure, the Fates and I know sacrifice greater than any being in this room. When you soldiers fall, you are blessed with death. When the Fates fail, we suffer a much greater loss." Anansi locked eyes with Shango as a figure emerged from the golden fountain at the Spider's back. It was Orunmila with a lifeless Ikenga in his arms. Two cousin-deities Shango had not seen since the early years of the Great War.

Orunmila stood tall with a placid face, still wielding that oak staff he favored beneath Ikenga's body. The Orisha's white beard was strong against his dark skin. He almost didn't seem alive, devoid of all expression. Even his green-and-yellow robes fell over his shoulders solemnly.

Ikenga appeared as a two-headed warrior, with one head facing forward and the other looking back. Both pairs of eyes were eerily devoid of life. His dead hands still gripped around a sword in one hand and a severed head in the other, each draped at his sides.

It was most surprising to Shango that Ikenga went along with the Fates instead of with the warriors. It was part of the reason Shango gave so much respect to the Fates initially. If someone like Ikenga who loved war the way he liked breathing went with them, who was Shango to question him? Now Shango wasn't so sure of that deference.

And it seemed as though Ikenga had suffered for that choice.

"What happened to Ikenga?" Oshosi asked, clearly worried about his cousin-deity. "Why is he limp in your arms like that, Orunmila?" It didn't even seem as though the Orisha was listening to him. "Orunmila, I am talking to you! Why have you left us to fend for ourselves? You let Ikenga's sword dull for too long and now... this. Explain yourselves! Thor deserves that much. Your curse with Time and Space be damned."

"Orunmila is not here to explain." Anansi approached the central podium, past the confused eyes of Magni and Modi. "Orunmila is here for me when I'm gone, as he is taking care of Ikenga now. This could've been avoided had this Divine Council heeded our warnings. Every time you dam the flow, we must sacrifice one from our ranks as well to keep it going, among the others I mentioned. We of the Fates edge closer and closer to a God Eater solution, nearly finding the perfect timeline, only to be undermined by you simple-minded warmongers." Anansi made sure to lock his sharp gaze on Shango, and Shango made a fist. "And this Justice Council with its very *fallible* wisdom." This time, his eyes were for the judges before he turned back to Shango. "Ikenga was the one to slice through your bifrost-lightning shaft as you came out of the End Realm. And you were right. I was the one weaving that message for you in the stars. That mortal of yours is sharp, thank the Heavens."

Shango bit back the retort he had ready. He'd already suspected it was partially his fault. If he had listened to Ayodeji sooner and taken the sign, he might've been able to return to help Thor, given him more time to fight off that vile serpent again. But it wouldn't have mattered if the Fates were going to meddle with his affairs, anyway.

"Tell the rest of Thor's story, Shango," Anansi demanded. "'Not one more step, brother,' is the next part. Am I right, cousin?"

Shango jumped from his seat, lashing out at the stone-faced Anansi.

18

The portal Shango crafted wasn't as neat as the one he had made with Ayodeji, but it would have to do. He had little of the bifrost left, and it would surely be spent. He didn't have time to use it gracefully, instead burning through it like a novice fire-maker ruining their flint. Oya complained as they slammed into the sides of the tight funnel several times.

"My bad," Shango apologized, "there's no time to make the tunnel big enough. We have to make do with my shoddy work."

Oya threw up an eyebrow, burgundy wraps whipping behind her. "My bad?"

"Apologies. Spent too much time with that mortal. He said it to me at least a dozen times an hour."

"All good, don't even sweat it." Oya winked. "Trust. I've been with these modern mortals longer than you have. Where is this place we're going, anyway? We already passed all our realms."

"To Ijọba Ipari. To the Great War. I'll explain later. I need you to help boost me."

Oya did her best, but it wasn't as good as what that mortal TJ had given Shango. The result lost them key moments Shango didn't have. He knew the importance of time in a war that was often decided by inches.

After too long a time for Shango's taste, the tunnel found its end.

"Push, Oya, push!" he commanded. Her Ashe was dwindling. He couldn't blame her. She had just fought Olokun and his armies almost single-handedly on that coastline. It was a wonder she could maintain herself at all. If Shango wasn't so single-minded in getting back to Thor, he would've smiled at his wife's utter vitality. She was "always down" as that boy Ayodeji would say, his "ride or die."

Gritting through her teeth, Oya said, "Just... a little... more!"

She didn't complain, never complained. Like a true warrior. She found a task, just as Shango did, and saw it to its bitter end. No matter the strain. He was a fool for wasting her talents in the Mortal Realm. It was utterly disrespectful.

With one last exertion of their dual wills, they broke through the plane of the End Realm. Shango had focused his mind on the Andromeda Front, where he would most likely find his brother-in-arms. And just before him was a sight straight out of a nightmare.

Thor's nightmare.

The Asgardian stood at the edge of the universe, broken asteroids and gas clouds backdropping his towering physique. His eyes were locked onto a massive serpent that lay before him atop a massive and unbroken asteroid.

Jörmungandr, the Midgard Serpent, twisted and snapped from a tear in reality.

How long the tear was open, Shango couldn't know. What he did know was that Thor was alone on that isolated asteroid, among too many corpses—Aplu and many other members of the Battalion among them. Shango had never seen so many deities laid to waste in one battle. A quick scan of the asteroid told of at least a dozen fallen warriors, deities and revenants alike. It was like a graveyard of spotted rainbow mist surrounding giants. And like an audience of pestering gnats, God Eater sentries encircled the melee.

Were the Eaters and Jörmungandr in a temporary alliance?

Were they using the giant serpent as their tool? Shango couldn't be sure.

Thor and Jörmungandr stood for a moment, sizing each other up. There were always moments like these in long-fought battles. A momentary gasp for breath before another round of fighting renewed. And in that instant, Thor caught sight of Shango from across the gas clouds. His expression, which had been infused with focus, softened to that trademarked smile. The smile that Shango had grown to admire from his old comrade.

Jörmungandr lunged forward, its jaws snapping shut. A single fang tore through Thor's arm, poison shooting straight through. The Asgardian roared to the heavens. Lightning streaks cast from his body instinctively, which forced Jörmungandr to stutter back. Thor's legs rocked under the weight of his body. His calves threatened to give out from beneath him.

"No!" Shango bellowed with great sorrow. "Hold your ground, brother! Hold your ground!"

But it was too late. The force of the blow sent Thor stumbling back three steps. Crimson blood leaked from his arm where the giant serpent got him. His arm nearly split in two.

Six more steps, Shango thought. *He has six more steps. There's still time.*

Shango and Oya landed on the edge of the asteroid. Shango's exhaustion was deep. All the Ashe he wasted that day was near to nothing. But he didn't allow that fatigue to enter his mind as he uplifted his axes. He shot two powerful bolts of red lightning into each of Jörmungandr's sickly yellow eyes. The God Eaters that encircled the asteroid took the hit and dissipated into mist. The remaining reformed to make a shadow barrier around Thor and the giant serpent.

"No!" Shango shouted as he shot more bolts from his axes. He blasted through, seeing glimpses of Thor desperately holding his ground, but the Eaters rebuilt their barriers soon after. Only faint lights of blue blossomed behind the shadow wall, followed by wails of shouting and deafening roars.

"Your bolts can't get through," Oya said at Shango's side, rolling her machete in hand and flinging her whip at her side, "but my winds can. I'll break up those shadows from behind, and then you can come through."

"Like that time we had to penetrate Aganju's volcano?"

Oya smiled and winked. "Just like that."

Shango nodded his affirmation, touching Oya on the shoulder to fill her with his lightning energy. His wife spun on her heel, whipping up electrified wind in her wake. Her dance quickly churned into a tornado of pulsating energy, and then she spiraled forward—straight into the black mass of the God Eater sentries. Unlike Shango, she did not push forth with the narrow focus of a lightning bolt, but with the ever-present permeation of wind. Where the Eaters tried to restore their border, she found an inch to slither through. Where the Eaters tried to attack her, she simply rotated on her heel like a leaf in the wind, her burgundy wrappings floating about her. It only took a few moments for her to get through and use her built-up charge to make way for Shango.

Smiling like the proud husband he was, Shango prepared his quads and calves to spring himself forward. Energy galvanized beneath his feet as he made ready a lightning bolt he could use to slide straight into the fight.

Hang on, Thor. We're coming.

"Now, Oya! Now!" Shango bellowed, and Oya used the charge he gave her to blast a hole through the God Eaters.

And there Thor was. Still alive. Blood leaking from too many holes in his body. And that giant serpent coming in for another strike.

Shango unleashed his tensed muscles and vaulted straight for the gap. Like Oya, he spiraled forward, making his body as narrow as possible, forcing his form briefly into a bolt of lightning. When he passed through the threshold, he unraveled himself, rolled into a crouch, and sent two bolts straight into the giant serpent's eye before it could chomp down on Thor. The impact sent shockwaves through the asteroid, but Jörmungandr merely shrieked in defiance.

"Oya!" Shango commanded. "Keep those shadows away from us. I'll make my way to Thor."

Oya nodded and stirred another tornado, keeping the Eaters away from the fight at the center of the asteroid. It almost looked like she was making a second inner shield against the God Eater's first one, not unlike the End Realm itself. Only now their battle was much smaller, one between two deities and a single monstrosity.

Jörmungandr drew back for another strike, snapping at Thor, who stood his ground well. But the giant serpent's strikes were much too fast. Thor was forced to sidestep the attack, narrowly avoiding the serpent's strikes. Two more steps taken.

He only has four more.

Keeping his knees locked in, Thor swung his mighty hammer and brought it crashing down onto the serpent's back.

Jörmungandr roared for only a moment, lightning pouring from its back. Under Oya's gray storm bubble, the blue light of the bolts enveloped them. They created a blanket of illumination all within the shadowy outer orb of the Eaters. The giant serpent whipped its head to Thor once more. Its neck curled back, making ready for a strike that would send Thor hurtling straight to his death. But before it could lash out, Shango threw himself before his friend, taking the blow for his brother instead.

The impact was like getting hammered by a raging comet. Ribs cracked under corded muscles. Ligaments tore over shattering bones.

And Shango didn't give a damn.

Before he knew it, the serpent was coiling around him, squeezing him tightly. Shango gritted his teeth, the unbroken bones in his back creaking under the pressure. But he refused to give in. With a surge of strength, he broke free of the serpent's grip and sent a bolt of lightning crackling through the air.

Jörmungandr recoiled, its scales smoking from the blast, but it wasn't done yet. Far from it. The serpent lunged forward again, jaws agape, and aimed at Shango. The Orisha leaped into the air, soaring over the serpent's head, and landed with a thunderous crash. He spun around, bringing his axes down with all his might, and struck the serpent in the side.

The blow was devastating. Jörmungandr writhed in agony. The whole asteroid shook as its body convulsed and it let out an ear-splitting roar. But it struck out with its impossibly long tail in retaliation. If Shango had been fresher and uninjured, he would've dodged it easily. Instead, he was hit full in the face and flung back into the rocks. Sharp stones carved into his back as he skidded backward. He only flew back a few dozen feet, though, stopped cold by a rock pillar.

Jörmungandr tasted the air with its tongue. It could sense the kill, Shango knew. The Orisha tried lifting from the pillar but his body was broken. He tried to summon lightning from his Ashe, but his spirit was dust.

Oya couldn't help, too preoccupied maintaining the bubble in her wind form. Thor had no steps to give; he was as good as dead.

They would all die here.

Just ahead of Shango, a mere four steps ahead and to the right, Thor huffed and puffed with his hammer gripped at his side. To the left, Jörmungandr approached for the final blow against Shango.

Damn Anansi. Damn Thor's orders.

Shango had trained for centuries to take on this beast, knew all its moves from Thor's stories. Had this been a fair fight, they would've defeated this monster like all the rest.

Thor and Shango exchanged a knowing look. The damned fool was going to save Shango, Shango knew it. In that split-second, he could see the mystical glow of lightning already filling his brother's eyes.

Shango shed an angry tear. "Not one more step, brother. Not one. Please."

But the fool just smiled and set off to save Shango's skin one last time.

One step, two steps, three steps, four.

Shango had thought he'd seen Thor's true strength before. They had shared countless battles with one another, after all. But that follow-up swing Thor committed to was beyond all reason. All natural laws of power were broken by Thor's Swan Song.

Like a swan, who was silent and gentle, everything Thor had done up to that point was merely a whisper. And like a dying swan singing a most beautiful and mournful song before death, Thor unleashed a well of power that lit the entire expanse around them, completely tearing through Oya's storm, the God Eater shield, all of it. And it gave way to the purple and blue clouds, painting the asteroid field around them in ultraviolet light.

From the dark, a star was born and died again, all within the scales of the Great Serpent, which could not contain the magic. Jörmungandr exploded in a fractured display of lightning bolts, torn into a thousand fried pieces. No remnants of its existence remained despite it stretching as long as the asteroid itself.

"Oya!" Shango called out. "Are you okay? Are you safe?"

"I'm okay!" she called from somewhere beyond, where the crags of the asteroid sizzled with Thor's last lightning attack. Her words were false, though, strained with pain. And her next words told the truth of it. "I'm just stuck under a rock... or four. I'll get out. Go to your friend!"

"No..." Shango left Thor's side and followed Oya's voice until he found her pinned between more than a dozen rocks that must've been loosed from Thor's blast. A few axe strikes broke the rocks apart, and he freed her. "I told you. I wouldn't leave you behind."

"But... Thor—"

"Is not my wife, is not my people."

With tears welling in her eyes, Oya wrapped her arms around Shango's neck. He winced from the pain but accepted the embrace all the same.

Thor coughed from behind. When Shango and Oya limped their way over to him, they could see that the Asgardian's skin was fried, his hair singed and blackened. Forgetting the pain in his arm, Shango reached out to his friend. He placed his palm along Thor's cheek. Somehow, despite being a breath away from death, the fool laughed. It was harsh and riddled with sick, but he laughed all the same. And then, without warning, the Mighty Thor's body stilled.

Shango had missed his final chance to speak to his friend. Now he went to a place Shango couldn't go. To Shango, it was as though he stood alone beneath the cosmic landscape, his heart heavy with an impossible grief. He shouted to the heavens and thunder echoed his sorrow, lightning mirrored his anguish. The only solace he could find within was that Thor had been blessed with a warrior's death. A good death. But the selfish part of Shango wanted to speak to him one last time.

Slowly, Oya knelt beside Shango. So quiet it was almost eerie. With a gentleness she did not often show, she drew her hand over Thor's opened eyes and closed them. Shango felt Ashe stir in Oya's belly. Some energy force he was not familiar with. Something not born of wind or lightning, but something else. That energy roiled in her mid-section, then shot to her usually glowing eyes. Only now her eyes were devoid of light, instead filled with the void of darkness.

"'*Don't you see it, Shango?*'" Oya said, but her voice was not entirely her own, layered with the timber of Thor's tonalities. Shango had nearly forgotten Oya could speak to the dead. "'*This is how it's meant to be. This is the destiny I have chosen. No more running from Jörmungandr. No more running from Fate. Remember your heart. Remember your woman, your people. Never forget them.*'" Oya tapped a shaking finger to Shango's temple, as though emulating the dying spirit of Thor within the ether. "'*This isn't your power.*'" Oya palmed Shango's chest. "'*This is your power. C'mon, Shango. Show me those pearly whites of yours. One last time.*'"

"You bastard." Shango's gritted teeth would have to do for a smile. "Don't go. Please don't go, brother."

Shango got no answer, for Oya's eyes went back to normal, and she wept. "I..." she started. "I saw his life flash before his eyes as he passed. H-He was a good friend, Shango. I'm glad you fought alongside him all this time. A-all the sacrifices you made... I understand now why you did it." She put a comforting arm over her husband's shoulder.

Shango had seen countless comrades who had fallen, but Thor was different. Entirely different. He thought he had readied himself for this moment; he couldn't be more wrong. Sadness poured into every inch of his body. Sorrow seeped into every crevice as he awkwardly hugged Thor's head.

"Shango..." Oya whispered. "Shango... there are others approaching in the distance."

Shango fixed his face, fear replacing grief instantly. "Go! Oya, you must run. It's the other deities. You're not registered; you're not under oath. They'll capture you."

Oya peeked over the smoldering horizon of the asteroid as she gathered a gas cloud. "No, I will not leave you. That's a wife's promise. Our oath goes both ways."

"I'm not going to lose you, too. I will see you again, but right now, you must run."

"No," she refused, and Shango could see now that others were indeed approaching. Many of them were already stitching the tear in reality made by Jörmungandr and the Eaters that were now all destroyed.

"There he is!" one of the deities said. Shango's vision was blurring. He wouldn't stay conscious for long. "Shango is right there."

"Hold him!" another shouted. "He abandoned his post for hours. He—"

"Stars, is that Thor?"

"I-it can't be. H-he's dead!"

With Jörmungandr obliterated, there was no scenario where the other deities would believe Shango.

"Stay away from him!" Oya roared. She attempted to fight them off, but she, like Shango, was far too exhausted to muster any real challenge. Through the haze of Shango's vision, he could barely make out her defeat. And in the end, the War Gods apprehended her, and both of them were carted off to the Court of All.

19

NOT ONE MORE STEP.

Those words pounded in Shango's mind as he re-lived Thor's last moments over again. And it was all Anansi's doing. He and his wretched Fates could've stopped it all. Shango would make him feel the pain that coursed through him. But he barely moved an inch in the Spider's direction before his mystical ribbons forced him back on the witness stand.

He couldn't move, but at least he could shout.

And that's what he did.

When all the breath left Shango's lungs, Anansi mockingly used his pinky to dig in his ear. "Do you see our power now, Council?" He ignored Shango's outburst entirely, which only redoubled the Orisha's fury. "We Fates are not playing tricks. This is absolutely serious. We—" Anansi cut himself off. His eyes had grown cloudy and gray and his sightline went just off to the side, as though he had lost sight of the Justice Council. "I don't have much time. The curse is taking hold. Blindness. Deafness. Then I'll lose the use of my limbs. Then my speech. Doomed to watch the end of all our stories without being able to help." Orunmila took a step forward, set Ikenga down on an empty bench, and approached Anansi's side to keep him from falling over. Was the Spider already losing the use of his limbs?

"We never questioned your omens and prophecies," Themis began, also ignoring Shango's rage. "We've only ever questioned your methods to achieve this end. And what you and the Fates have subjected yourselves to, we would never do to ourselves."

"Thor's death was always fated and written," Anansi confessed. "It was an unchanging and inevitable event. We just forced it forward in the timeline to prevent something far worse, or have you all forgotten the enemy we are facing now?" Anansi collapsed to his knees, and he jabbed at his ears. His next words came out as an awkward shout. Deafness must've befallen him. "We had to prove what we are doing is right. That the status quo needs to change while we still have the power to affect the outcome. We are at a grand crossroad." He twisted his head wildly to the whole of the courtroom, racing against whatever curse was coursing through him faster and faster. "You all are concerned with the fact that Thor is dead, when instead you should be worrying about how a powerful being like Jörmungandr was twisted by the latest reality tear. We warned that the game would change like this. The God Eaters aren't going to always attack as a blunt-force enemy. First, it was the mind-rakers, now the corrupters. Soon, it'll be total damnation. And my sacrifice will prove the commitment of the Fates. So listen to my final words: Call the mortal boy, TJ Young, Tomori Jomiloju Young, to the stand."

Themis snarled for the first time that day. "But why!? Give us a straight answer!"

"That's all we have, as far as we could see through the veil. If we had more time, we could have a more concrete answer. But..." Anansi coughed, as though choking on ash. "He is our last hope against this Sovereign Threat. He is the literal key to seal the End Realm for another thousand years... His path is—"

And then Anansi's voice left him completely. Nothing more than a mute.

Shango watched in horror as the once vibrant and mischievous deity became nothing more than an empty husk of his former self. The festering magic devoured his essence like smoke, like a God Eater. It slithered through his eyes, his nose, his mouth. Then it left him and drifted into the air as though it hadn't just defiled the divine body of a god. Orunmila, still stoic as ever, still not saying a word, lifted Anansi to his shoulder. Then he went for Ikenga as well and did the same. He was now the last of the trio, these cousin-deities. With two lifeless bodies slumped against him, Orunmila made his way back to the central fountain. And there he dipped into the golden pool and vanished, leaving the whole courtroom in awe.

Devastation racked Shango's body. So much power had been lost in such a short time. All because he *briefly* left the End Realm. But a new thought came to his mind.

He realized then that the Great Separation might have been a mistake. Oya was so much stronger when she interacted with the mortals. He felt as powerful as ever with the humans as well, to the point where some boy manifested some power greater than he had ever known.

Thor said to follow his heart. And that's what he would do from here on out. He needed to pledge himself to his people wholly and honestly. Not abandon the End Realm, but reestablish what was lost with his people so that he may be better prepared for the shadows to come. Shango stood up and spoke. "Esteemed Judges, Anansi is right. We are at a crossroads. And I believe it's time that we—I... reconnect with the Mortal Realm—"

Oshosi waved a frantic hand in the air. "Ah! Um.. May I call for a moment with my charge?" he asked, stomping to Shango and piercing him with a whisper. "You're practically *asking* for the Channeling now. What in the Three Realms are you doing?"

"What I should have done long ago," Shango said. "Listen to the cries of our people, find strength with our own as we did in times past. I can no longer pledge myself fully to the End Realm...

or else..." He pointed to where Anansi fell. "We'll all end up like our cousin there."

Oshosi groaned. "No, no, no, we will *not* be doing that, not with *this* court. Give me one more chance to fix things."

"I'm not changing my mind on this one, old friend." He paused. "I must follow my heart as Thor advised me to. And my heart is with my people. But... this better be good."

Oshosi turned on his heel and addressed the court, clearing his throat to say, "So... um... Esteemed Judges. May I request a recess to retrieve this TJ Young?"

Embark on an extraordinary journey with TJ Young, a seemingly ordinary teenager from Los Angeles, as he uncovers the mystical world of the West African Orishas.

This riveting young adult fantasy series delves into a realm where magic intertwines with destiny, and ancient secrets are waiting to be unearthed.

In the heart of modern-day Los Angeles, TJ Young, raised in a secret community of gifted, magical diviners, is thrust into a world of magic and mystery following his sister's enigmatic death in Nigeria. His quest for answers leads him to Camp Olosa in New Orleans and eventually to the prestigious Ifa Academy for Tomorrow's Diviners in West Africa. Each step of his journey brings him closer to powerful spirits and gods, forcing him to navigate a path filled with danger, loyalty, and the stark reality of what it means to make promises to deities.

visit this link:
https://www.antoinebandele.com/an-old-gods-story

GLOSSARY

- **Aganju:** a deity in Yoruba religion and African diaspora traditions like Candomblé and Santería, known as the god of volcanoes, the wilderness, and the Earth's molten core, often represented as a powerful and authoritative figure associated with transformation and strength.
- **Ammit:** a mythological creature from ancient Egyptian belief, often referred to as the "Devourer of the Dead," responsible for consuming the hearts of the deceased if they were found unworthy during the judgment of their souls.
- **Anansi:** a well-known character and deity in African and Caribbean folklore, often portrayed as a cunning and clever spider who is a trickster figure, known for his ability to outsmart others and navigate tricky situations using wit and guile.
- **Aplu:** also known as Apollo in Greek mythology, he is a significant god associated with various aspects, including the sun, music, prophecy, healing, and archery, often depicted as a youthful and handsome

figure, and widely venerated in ancient Greece and beyond.

- **Asgardian:** citizens and inhabitants of Asgard, a mythical realm in Norse mythology inhabited by powerful gods and beings, including the likes of Thor and Odin.
- **Ashe:** the inherent force of all creation and magic, including primal power and creative potential.
- **Bifrost:** a mythical rainbow bridge in Norse mythology that connects the realm of the gods, Asgard, to the realm of humans, Midgard, and is often portrayed as a shimmering, multicolored bridge that is guarded by the god Heimdall.
- **Chaac:** an ancient Maya deity in Mesoamerican mythology, recognized as the god of rain, thunder, and agriculture, often depicted with a prominent serpent-like nose, symbolizing his association with life-giving rainfall.
- **Eshu:** the Messenger Orisha, the Gatekeeper, or the Trickster, characterized by his jovial natured paired with deep wisdom.
- **Forseti:** a Norse god in Germanic mythology, known as a deity of justice, peace, and reconciliation, often depicted as a wise and fair judge who settles disputes and promotes harmony among gods and humans.
- **Gleipnir:** a mythical chain or binding in Norse mythology, famously created to restrain the monstrous wolf Fenrir, known for its incredible strength and the unusual materials used in its construction.
- **Greystone:** the magical insinuation for the inhabits of Norway.
- **Heimdall:** a mythological figure in Norse mythology, known as the guardian of the Bifrost bridge, possessing extraordinary senses and vigilance,

often depicted as a watchful deity with the duty of protecting the realm of the gods.

- **Hel:** a figure associated with the realm of the dead, also known as "Helheim," where souls of the deceased go after death if they did not die in battle, and she is typically depicted as a half-living, half-dead being, overseeing this afterlife realm.
- **Ibeji:** the Twin Orishas, characterized as rambunctious, childlike spirits that are full of youthful fun.
- **Ifa:** a prominent system of divination and religious belief rooted in Yoruba culture, primarily practiced by the Yoruba people of West Africa, which involves the consultation of sacred texts and divination tools to seek guidance, wisdom, and solutions to life's challenges, including spiritual and practical matters.
- **Ikenga**: two-faced Ikenga is the oldest concept of Ikenga in Igboland. It is a two-faced god, with one face looking at the old year while one face looks at the new year. This is the basis of the oldest and most ancient Igbo calendar
- **Issitoq:** a deity that punishes those who break taboos. He usually takes the form of a giant flying eye.
- **Jörmungandr:** a monstrous serpent or sea serpent in Norse mythology, also known as the Midgard Serpent or World Serpent, said to encircle the world, biting its own tail, and destined to play a significant role in the events of Ragnarök, where it battles the god Thor and contributes to the world's destruction.
- **Khaos:** in Greek mythology, he represents the primordial void or chaos from which the universe and everything in it emerged, symbolizing the formless state that predated the creation of the world.

- **Ma'at:** an ancient Egyptian concept and goddess associated with truth, balance, order, justice, and harmony, serving as a foundational principle in Egyptian religion and culture, often depicted as a woman with an ostrich feather on her head, and the weighing of one's heart against the feather of Ma'at is a central element in the Egyptian afterlife judgment.
- **Medjay:** an ancient people of Nubia (in modern-day Sudan) who served as a paramilitary and police force in ancient Egypt during various periods of its history, known for their skills in desert warfare and their role in maintaining order and protecting Egypt's borders.
- **Midgar:** in Norse mythology, is the realm of humans, situated at the center of the cosmos and separated from other worlds by the great serpent Jörmungandr, representing the inhabited Earth
- **Mithra:** a deity from ancient Indo-Iranian and Zoroastrian religions, and later, Mithraism, a mystery religion in the Roman Empire, known as a god of light, truth, and contracts, often depicted slaying a bull and associated with cosmic and moral order.
- **Mjölnir:** a mythical weapon in Norse mythology, famously associated with the Norse god Thor, depicted as a powerful and enchanted hammer capable of causing thunder and lightning, and it is a symbol of Thor's strength and protection.
- **Ijọba Ipari:** the Yoruba word for the "End Realm", an ethereal plane outside of conventional space and time, which houses the Great War against the God Eaters.
- **Inanna:** an ancient Mesopotamian goddess, known as the Sumerian counterpart to the Akkadian goddess Ishtar, associated with love, fertility, beauty, sex, war, and other aspects of life, and her stories and myths are

prominent in Sumerian literature, including the famous "Descent of Inanna" narrative.

- **Jigoku:** a Japanese term that translates to "hell" in English, referring to the concept of the afterlife realm of punishment and suffering in various Buddhist and Shinto belief systems, where souls are judged and face the consequences of their actions.
- **King Impulu:** the leader of the impundulu, mythical creatures in Zulu folklore and southern African mythology, often described as a large, supernatural birds or lightning birds, believed to have the ability to summon thunderstorms and associated with witchcraft and omens in the culture.
- **Kohl:** a cosmetic product, often in the form of a dark powder or paste, traditionally used in various cultures, including Middle Eastern, South Asian, and North African, to outline and enhance the eyes, serving both cosmetic and cultural purposes.
- **Lugh:** a prominent god in Celtic mythology, revered for his multifaceted talents and roles, including being a god of craftsmanship, arts, and warfare.
- **Obatala:** the Architect Orisha, the Healer, or the Shepard of the Imperfect, characterized by his gentle personality and eternal patience.
- **Olodumare:** the Almighty Orisha, the Father, or the omnipotent, characterized by his great power and all-knowing pools of knowledge. He is all things.
- **Olokun:** the Orisha of the Deep Blue, the Ruler of the Seas. Husband to Yemoja, and parent to most other water Orishas.
- **Olosa:** the Lagoon Orisha, characterized for her abundance, prosperity, and fertility.
- **Òlòṣí:** the Yoruba word for "bastard" or "foolish person."

- **Orishas:** a group of deities and spirits in the Yoruba religion, which originated in West Africa and is practiced in various forms in the African diaspora, particularly in the Caribbean and the Americas, with each Orisha representing different aspects of nature, human experiences, and divine forces, and they play a central role in religious ceremonies and cultural traditions.
- **Orunmila:** the Orisha of the Cosmos, the Ruler of the Stars, characterized by his righteousness and wisdom. One of the few Orishas to witness the Creation Event.
- **Oshosi:** the Orisha of the Hunt, characterized by his serious nature and deep patience, though those traits have seemingly been cast aside as of late.
- **Oshun:** the Orisha of Rivers, characterized by her sensuality, love, and purity. One of the wives of Shango.
- **Owuo:** the deity of Death in the Asante and Akan mythology of West Ghana and the Ewe.
- **Oya:** the Orisha of Storms, the Windweaver, characterized by her tenacity and compassion. One of the wives of Shango.
- **Oyo:** historically refers to an ancient Yoruba kingdom and empire located in what is now modern-day Nigeria, known for its rich history and cultural heritage, including its significant impact on the spread of Yoruba culture, religion, and political influence across West Africa.
- **Perun:** a god in Slavic mythology, particularly in East Slavic and Baltic traditions, often associated with thunder, lightning, and war, and is regarded as a powerful and revered deity in the pantheon, playing a significant role in early Slavic beliefs.

- **Raijin**: a mythical figure in Japanese folklore and religion, often depicted as a fearsome deity or demon associated with thunder, lightning, and storms, and is sometimes portrayed with drums to create thunder, symbolizing the power and unpredictability of natural forces.
- **Ragnarök:** a cataclysmic event in Norse mythology, often referred to as the "Twilight of the Gods," where a series of apocalyptic events, including battles and natural disasters, lead to the end of the world and the eventual rebirth of the cosmos in a new cycle.
- **Raijū**: a legendary creature in Japanese folklore, often described as a shape-shifting, lightning-imbued animal, such as a wolf, fox, or weasel, believed to be a companion to Raijin, the god of thunder, and sometimes causing lightning strikes by entering the bodies of trees or humans during thunderstorms.
- **Shango:** the Thunder Orisha, the Lionhearted, or The Overseer of Masculinity and Masculine Beauty, characterized by his loud personality and substantial presence.
- **Utenheim:** the Norse word for the "End Realm", an ethereal plane outside of conventional space and time, which houses the Great War against the God Eaters.
- **Yamaraja:** in Hindu mythology, he is the lord of death and the king of the afterlife, responsible for judging souls and determining their fate in the cycle of reincarnation, also known as the god of dharma (righteousness) and justice.
- **Yemoja:** the mother of all Orishas. The Orishas of creation, water, motherhood, and moonlight.

ALSO BY ANTOINE BANDELE

TJ & THE ORISHAS

The Gatekeeper's Staff

The Windweaver's Storm

The Hero's Equinox

ORISHAS AMONG MORTALS

Will of the Mischief Maker

When the Wind Speaks

An Axe for a Hammer

TALES FROM ESOWON

The Kishi

THE SKY PIRATE CHRONICLES

By Sea & Sky

Of Ruin & Silk

LOST TALES FROM ESOWON

Last of My Kind

Stoneskin

ANTHOLOGIES

Orishas Among Mortals

Demons, Monks, & Lovers

Tales from the Otherworlds

The Chronicles of Underrealm

ABOUT THE AUTHOR

Antoine lives in Los Angeles, CA with his life partner and cat. He is a YouTuber, producing work for his own channel, which mostly covers *Avatar: The Last Airbender*.
He is also an audiobook engineer.

Whenever he has the time, he's writing books inspired by African folklore, mythology, and history.

antoinebandele.com

www.ingramcontent.com/pod-product-compliance
Lightning Source LLC
Chambersburg PA
CBHW020333310726
48979CB00015B/2350/J

9781951905385